DISCARD

500 numbered and 15 lettered copies of
MOTHERLESS CHILD have been printed.

This is copy

110

GLEN HIRSHBERG

MOTHERLESS CHILD

# GLEN HIRSHBERG

# MOTHERLESS CHILD

earthling publications • halloween 2012

FIRST EDITION, FIRST PRINTING
October 2012

ISBN-13: 978-0-9838071-1-7

EARTHLING PUBLICATIONS
P.O. Box 413
Northborough, MA 01532 USA
Email: earthlingpub@yahoo.com
Website: www.earthlingpub.com

Author's website: http://www.glenhirshberg.com

Printed in the U.S.A.

For Kate, Sid, and Kim, with a road to ride,

and a mixtape to play (louder than you want me to)

*Redemption is never impossible and always equivocal.*

—Ellen Willis

# PART ONE

## Do Run

## Run

She met him on a Monday. Her heart stood still. At the time, she was sure his did, too. Of course, she turned about to be right about that.

The place was called the Back Way Out, a uniquely Charlotte sort of shithole, tricked out like a real juke joint with crooked shingles hammered over the drywall and sawdust shavings scattered across the stain-resistant vinyl-and-tile flooring. The Gimmick, even more than the décor, gave the bar away as the young banker-haven it was: everyone who entered got a laminated, folding yellow card, with a clip-art sketch of a beer mug on it and 87 tiny squares. Fill each square by drinking — or at least ordering — all 87 varieties of microbrew the bar served, and you became a Back Way Out legend and got your photo on the Crossroads Wall behind the stage. Fill 43 squares, and you got a yellow *Halfway Out the Back* T-shirt, complete with drooling smiley-face logo.

Natalie considered it a small sign of hope for humanity that she saw at least half a dozen drooling smiley-face T-shirts as Sophie dragged her through the door but no new photos on the Crossroads Wall. The last time they'd come, eighteen months before, there'd been the same three grinning frat-boy idiots up there, in matching oversized Hornets jerseys. *Eighteen months*, Natalie found herself wondering? *Was that really all?* It seemed so much longer. Way back in their old lives. Back when they'd had lives. Now, she just wanted to go home.

She held up her cellphone. "I'm going to go call them," she said, wincing as the guy in the Stetson on the stage unleashed a feedback shriek while trying to tune his guitar.

"It's not really halfway," Sophie said, cocking her hip and folding her hands under her breasts so that they surfaced in the V of her summer dress. Right on cue, half a dozen pairs of beer-glazed eyes swung in her direction.

Natalie rubbed a tired hand over her face. She'd taken her longest shower in over a year before coming out tonight, combed and given a curl to her hair, which was still new-road black even if she hadn't had it cut in months, applied actual perfume for the first time since forever. And still, she smelled like Johnson & Johnson.

"Excuse you?" she said.

"43. Isn't really halfway to 87."

"It's a convenient stop on the road to Moronville."

"Spoken like you've been there," Sophie said. She'd loosened her arms, let her breasts dip just far enough back into the V to draw at least a few of those beer-glazed gazes upward, and now she was having fun locking eyes with everyone. "It's not their fault, after all. They're not the ones went and got themselves knocked up."

"That's because they're…" Natalie started, caught the glance of one bespectacled, boots-sporting pretend-cowboy who'd gone straight past Sophie to her, and felt herself blush. Did she really look decent in this dress anymore? 24 years old, and she already felt like a mom who'd donned a cheerleader costume in the hopes of feeling sexy again. Except Sophie'd been the cheerleader. And Johnson & Johnson wasn't sexy, no matter what dress it was wearing. Only the mom part was right.

"I'm going to check on our children," she said.

"Watch this." Sophie pulled her arms in tight again, grinning as the poor bankers' chins dipped. "It's like playing beach ball with seals."

"Two beach balls," Natalie muttered, and Sophie laughed.

"There's my Nat."

"Where?" Natalie said, and moved off toward the hallway by the restrooms to get some relative quiet.

When she came back ten minutes later, Sophie was sitting at a table near the stage with three guys in loosened ties, her unknotted blond hair spilling artfully over her shoulder. In front of her sat three separate umbrella drinks, each a different shade of day-glo.

"Saved one for you," Sophie chirped.

Natalie stared down at her oldest friend, flushed and smiling and still nowhere near pre-pregnancy weight and not caring. Then she stared at the drinks, then the guys Sophie had collected. One of them bald, another black. Clean, pleasant faces, well-shaven or meticulously unshaven. On the right, farthest from Sophie, sat the spectacle-guy who'd eyed her before. He was eying her still, shyly. He'd pushed back far enough from the table that Natalie could just see the Kenneth Cole messenger bag leaning against his right boot. In spite of herself, and her now-perpetual exhaustion, and her own mother's voice still echoing in her ears—"*Your babies are fine, Nat, God's sakes. Have a hard one on me*"— she felt herself nod.

"What if I want two?"

"*There's* my Nat," Sophie said, slapping the table while the black guy blinked and the bald guy trembled and Spectacle-banker's eyes went just a bit wider.

The musician onstage was strictly Advanced Karaoke, perfect for a training-wheel New South bar like the Back Way Out, but he had some taste, at least: "Thousand Miles from Nowhere," "Sally Sue Brown." Spectacle-guy, once he got up the nerve to sprinkle in some conversation with the shy glances, turned out to be enough of a Baltimore Orioles fan to have recognized Merv Rettenmund in a truck stop once, which Natalie figured qualified him, at the very least, to hear her Dave McNally hiccough story a little later in the evening. After some dancing. If he could dance. She had her fingers curled around a tallboy, her head cocked just enough so she could hear Sophie's laughter over the music and Spectacle-guy's increasingly animated, friendly chatter, and had finally remembered what it was—besides the boys, the beautiful, pitiful, sweating, shining boys—that she really had almost loved about all this, when the lights went out.

They went all at once, as if there'd been a power outage, or someone had flipped a switch. As it turned out, that's what had happened, because of course, the Back Way Out had no dimmers, no spotlight, wasn't set up for anything other than the game almost anyone who ever walked through its doors imagined they were playing. One row of track lights—the wrong one, too far back near the bar—blinked back on, then off again. Then the row over the stage, right above their table, and Natalie squinted.

"Holy shit," she murmured. Spectacle-guy hadn't even turned around, wasn't curious, was too hell bent on getting to her. Which of course doomed him, as far as Natalie was concerned. Then she stopped thinking about him entirely.

"Whoa," said Sophie, one hand grasping the black guy's forearm. "You see that? He just—"

"Ladies and gentlemen," boomed a gravelly woman's voice from the back, "we hope you appreciate the gravity of your good fortune."

The new figure onstage really seemed simply to have appeared, a junkie-thin scarecrow all in black, complete with button-up work shirt, unlaced, half-collapsed hiking boots that looked more like potatoes than shoes, and a completely incongruous sombrero that mashed his dark hair down around his face. His narrow nose tilted to the right, and his fingers seemed to tremble slightly as he sketched a wave at the drinkers of the Back Way Out and then slid his hands deep into his pants pockets. Natalie took all of that in but soon found herself staring at his mouth, which looked too rounded, the lips forming a near-perfect circle.

"He looks like a blow-up doll," Sophie whispered in her ear, hitting a simile exactly right, for once. Then she added, "With a leak," and Natalie wanted to hug her, and also to cry, but she didn't know why.

"You know who that is, right?" She watched the guitarist shift, straighten his Stetson, and go still, apparently awaiting some communication from his new companion.

"I know you do," said Sophie.

"It's the Whistler. It has to be."

"No shit."

"Who's the Whistler?" said Spectacle-guy, and Sophie stuck her index finger to his lips and shook her head.

"Dude," she said.

What had Natalie expected them to play? Some George Jones wallow, maybe. One of the Blue Yodels. Something that let the Whistler communicate just how lonesome-sorry he was, since that's what he was famous for amongst the truckers who came into the Waffle House where Natalie worked nights and the handful of music-nerd friends from her two years at UNCC who'd spirited her off on weekend jaunts into western Georgia, down to Lake Charles Louisiana, in search of the ghosts and echoes of what they called the "real stuff." As if ghosts and echoes were the closest to real anyone could get anymore. Her friends, she realized, would have been at once electrified and horrified to discover the Whistler at the Back Way Out.

The Whistler cleared his throat, shivered his bony shoulders. Natalie half-expected stalks of straw to poke out through his buttonholes. Then he muttered low to the guitarist, who swayed in place. Broke into a dazed smile, as if he couldn't believe his luck.

"Well, y'all," he said and tuned his e-string again, even though it was already in tune. "I never thought I'd get a chance to do this. With this man."

And then he broke into "Red Cadillac and a Black Mustache." Too slow, at first, which agitated Natalie even more than it should have, until the Whistler glanced, just once, at the guitarist. The tempo picked up. Then more. As though the guy were a gas pedal, and the Whistler had floored him. The whole room began to clap and shudder. Even before the Whistler pulled those pursed lips just a little tighter, preparing, Natalie knew she was in trouble.

"Pretty sure who *that guy'll* be loving, anyway," Sophie half-sang along, elbowing Natalie under her rib cage as the guitar chugged and the melody hit full gallop.

"Yeah. Me, too," Natalie murmured back. Followed by, "I mean, shut up."

But the Whistler had spotted her, now. No. Had been looking at her from the second he'd slipped from the shadows. Had never, for one moment, looked elsewhere. Even as he pulled in breath and held it, she saw the edges of his mouth stretch toward smiling.

"Uh-oh," she said, holding the table.

The Whistler let loose.

Later—so much later, dawn a red rip in the skin of the dark and birds already stirring in the poplars of whatever-the-hell park they'd parked Sophie's Kia beside—Natalie awoke face-down in a spill of blood atop someone's bare stomach. Sophie's stomach, she realized, sat up too fast, and grabbed the back of the front passenger seat as the world tilted over and the half a beer she was almost sure was all she'd drunk shot up her throat. Even before the world steadied, she cried out, touched her fingers to the dried redness streaked across Sophie's abdomen and trailing into her belly button and up under her bare breasts. She shook her friend hard and realized, just as Sophie blinked awake, that there were no wounds she could see. *Which meant the blood was hers?*

She frantically checked her own skin but found nothing of note except that it was bare, too. The shreds of her dress she located around her waist.

Sophie sat up, cringing against even the faint light just spreading along the horizon. She ran a hand over herself, shoulder to hip, noted the blood, looked at Natalie. To Natalie's astonishment, she smiled. Sleepily. "Hey," she said.

"Jesus Christ, Sophie." Natalie pulled enough of her dress together to shrug it partially closed around her shoulders. "Did we...?"

"Pretty sure," Sophie murmured, not bothering to cover any part of herself except her eyes.

"Both of us? With him? With the Whistler? How the…how did *that* happen?" For a long moment, they just sat. The light and the birdsong needled at Natalie, too, and she winced and closed her eyes. "Could we go home now? To our children?"

"What'd you do to my dress?" Sophie said, trying to find enough buttons to close herself.

They got out of the car, settled into the front seats. Even with the motor running, Natalie still imagined she could hear birds, a shrill warble driving up her ear canals toward her brain. "Was that me? Did we really do that? *Why?*"

The clock on Sophie's radio read 4:45, too early for even the early bird rush hour, and they passed unaccompanied and unobserved down the empty, tree-lined streets of suburban Charlotte, past the rows-upon-rows of pines and poplars and perfectly mown lawns and subdivision signs. *The Oaks. The Hill. Oak Tree Hill.*

"I don't remember a goddamn thing," Natalie said. But that wasn't true. It was coming back. Bits and flashes. The Whistler at their table with his pursed mouth and his sombrero-mashed hair, smiling sadly down at his hands, which trembled on the table like a butterfly he'd caught. That woman appearing behind him. Pearl-wearing, pinch-faced African American woman, grandmotherly glasses, rumpled green skirt-suit, disapproving frown. The three of them—Natalie, Sophie, the

Whistler—in the car—in this car—much later. Sophie's soft lips against Natalie's own. Their hands up each other's dresses. The Whistler still there. *Where?*

Natalie closed her eyes against the light and the woozy whirl of half-memory. She put her hands to her ears, but that didn't help. When she opened her eyes, Sophie was squinting at her, holding up a shielding hand against the sliver of sun just peeking over the edge of the earth as they neared Honeycomb Corner, the trailer park where Natalie had grown up.

"You know," Sophie said quietly, steering with one hand, pulling her tangled hair straight with the other, "I always kind of wanted to do that." She glanced toward Natalie. "With you. Stop looking like that, why is that so shocking?" She looked away.

Natalie blinked, winced, shook her head. "It's not…it's just…you did? I mean, you have?"

"Kind of. Yeah. I don't know." She turned back to Natalie. And there was her smile. The ghost of it, fleeting and sad. "I like you."

She turned the Kia off Sardis into the dirt, and they jostled down the rutted track, between silent, rusting trailers hunched in their berths like pre-fab mausoleums. The curtains all drawn, doors shut, no one moving, nothing living. Always, even in mid-day, with Skynyrd blasting out of the new hairy dirt-bike family's window and laundry drooping on dipping lines and people shouting at other people to shut up and kids smoking out by the perimeter fence or racing bikes up the dirt ruts and adults smoking everywhere, this place had always reminded Natalie more of a cemetery than a neighborhood.

Sophie parked in the shade of Natalie's mother's double-wide. They sat together just a little longer, staring out the windshield, until Natalie said, "Soph? Are you sure...I mean, what, exactly did we do?"

To Natalie, it sounded as though she were speaking through water. Sophie's movements seemed submerged, too, a slow sweep of her hand up her ruined dress, a long shrug. "I don't know, Nat," she said, so softly. "But it hurt."

After that, Natalie stumbled inside and straight into her bed with that sound in her ears, blaring but from far, far away, like a tornado warning from another county.

**Smiled at the Kitty.**

**Petted It.**

*After he released them, left them sleeping one atop the other in the backseat of the car, his Destiny and her companion, he went walking in the woods. The air tasted salty in his teeth when he remembered to taste it, but the heat had already begun evaporating through his pores. By the time he emerged from the trees onto some other main road, he could feel the shivers starting again in his ankles, along his spine. Under a streetlight, in the middle of the empty street, he held up his hands. They, at least, looked steady for now. So enjoyable, this feeling, every time it came. The Need.*

*Except that this time…had he really done it? Of course he had, he'd made sure before he left them.* How *had he done it?* How *did it happen? He had no idea. Remembered, vaguely, Mother telling him she didn't know either. That none of them did. When it was time…when you found your One…the power just…came.*

*By the tilt of the earth beneath his feet and the shade of black overhead, he knew he had only an hour or two. Soon, he'd have to call Mother, so she could pick him up. She wouldn't be happy. Would upbraid him mercilessly, because she didn't understand, yet. Didn't know that their time together was ending. That he'd found his Destiny, after all these years. The thought that she didn't know somehow made it all even better. An hour ago, as he'd realized what was occurring, he wouldn't have considered that possible.*

*His Destiny. He'd seen her first the night before, through the Waffle House window, juggling syrup bottles and plates as she danced between tables, not even knowing she was dancing. He'd slipped away from Mother and spent hours and hours watching. Listening to her sing her way, slump-shouldered and exhausted, to her car in the wee hours. Watching her settle on the stoop of her trailer in the early summer moonlight, her hair coming loose and her tired chin down on her neck and her child, which she'd gone into the trailer to fetch, in her arms.*

*Abruptly, the trembles hit him again, viciously. Usually, after a Feed, he got weeks, sometimes months before he felt so much as a prickle of hunger. But of course, he hadn't actually fed, this time. Not completely. Not yet. Despite the trembles. Despite the Need. For his Destiny's sake. Because that's how strong his love was.*

*That's how strong his love was.*

*He caught the melody, clung to it, swayed to it right there on the double yellow line. If a truck came, he'd throw his arms open to it, embrace it like a lover. Because he would love it. Did in fact love it all. That's what Mother had forgotten. How to love it all. That's why he could not stay.*

23

*He felt tears of gratitude in his eyes, a swelling in his chest—for his Destiny, he knew, not for Mother—and he threw back his head, sucked the night in and in and in, pursed his lips, let the shivers and the long, empty, lonely years roll up him. And then he let them out, like steam screaming through a kettle.*

*When he did call, Mother answered immediately. "Just stay right there," she snapped.*

*"Don't be mad," he said, careful to disguise his laughter, moving to the curb to hunker down with his arms around himself so the shudders didn't shake him apart. "I'm so cold."*

*"You don't know what you've done. Hell, I don't know what you've done."*

*"Did you see her? Mother?" the Whistler said. Shuddering. Holding himself together.*

*"I saw her."*

*"Where are you?"*

*"Coming. Close. What'd you do with the other one?"*

*"Left her. Of course."*

*Silence. Over the chattering of his teeth and the rattle in his bones, the Whistler thought he could hear Mother's truck. Then, "You must be freezing."*

*The Whistler could see her headlights, like giant, judging eyes. "I'll be warm soon," he whispered.*

*If she heard, she didn't answer. And if she understood…*

*If she understood, he thought—and he couldn't fight the smile now—she'd just keep going. Never look back.*

*Instead, just as he knew she would, she pulled up beside him, climbed out, and helped him hoist his shivering, teary-eyed, smiling self into the cab of the truck.*

## Shake. Rattle.

## Roll.

When did Natalie know?

Not at first, waking up with her bones sore and her eyes itching but her head surprisingly clear, reaching for the digital clock by the bed and seeing it was after ten and then catching a shard of moonlight across the back of her palm and hearing the Orioles broadcast from the stoop in front of the trailer. That flat, familiar voice chanting, "*Out* at the plate." *So, ten at night?*

She shot upright, calling, "Eddie? *Eddie*?"

"You want to wake him, shut up," her mother snapped, reentering through the trailer's open screen door, resting her radio and the Burger King glass containing her nightly mint-lemonade on the square of countertop next to the sink.

Natalie's eyes swung to the folding bassinet that served as Eddie's crib. There he was, her little caterpillar boy, curled in his blue blanket with his amazing hair every which way, a thousand little antennas pulling in the world, even in his sleep. She stood, winced, stretched, leaned over the bassinet.

"Thanks, Mom," she said. Eddie's cheeks felt warm, not feverish but so warm, and she held her fingers to them as though over a fire. When she glanced up, her mother was sipping her lemonade, leaning against the doorframe.

"*Strike* three called, right down the middle," said the radio.

"Crap," Jess said, folding her arms and somehow settling even deeper into the floppy blue cardigan she put on every single evening, the second she got home. Her ankle-scraper of a skirt draped her like a lampshade and made her look even shorter. "Eight-nothing, bottom of the 8th." She looked up at Natalie, and just for a moment, behind her big, round glasses, her eyes flashed. Tiny, blue, and deadly. Little switchblades.

Natalie sang her the Mr. Rogers song anyway, as she always did at the sight of that cardigan.

"Shut up," her mother said.

"I'll be your neighbor."

"Yeah, well, what should I sing you? 'Drinkin' Wine Spo-dee-O-Dee?'"

"You can sing it," Natalie mumbled. "You'd be wrong, though."

"You look…" Jess started, then stopped. The switchblades flashed again. On the radio, David Ortiz hit another shot out of Camden Yards, and her mother shut off the game.

Natalie's gaze kept wandering from her sleeping son to her mom to the window. She swayed on her feet, feeling strange. Too light. Sort of sick. And like she wanted to throw her mother aside, bolt out the door, and run. Not to get away, not to go anywhere. Just to move.

"Go on," she said.

Jess shrugged, lowered her eyes, went back to looking like a lawn gnome. "Less awful than you should. What happened to you last night?"

Natalie started toward the counter to brew coffee before realizing she didn't want any. Pulling off the T-shirt she suspected her mother had somehow slipped on her while she slept—over the shreds of her dress—she edged into the bathroom to change into her work uniform, and to hide her embarrassment. Eventually, she said, "I'm on at 11."

When she emerged, her mother was sitting in a folding chair at the square folding table. She'd poured Natalie some cereal. Natalie shook her head, ran a brush through her hair.

"Maybe you shouldn't go in tonight, hon."

Natalie nodded. "You might be right. Or I might be fine. I actually can't tell."

"Have something to eat."

"I don't want anything."

Instead of arguing, Jess watched her finish dressing. The moonlight seemed to etch her there, by herself. For almost fifteen years, ever since Natalie's father's death, her mother had been alone. Because she'd never gotten over it. Because she dressed like Mr. Rogers. Or because her clothes could soften but never disguise her. *Not many men in the trailer park know how to ride a mustang when they spot one,* as her mother liked to put it.

She was holding her Burger King glass to her lips, now, and she looked, incongruously, like a little girl playing Mr. Microphone. A little girl who'd given up her whole life to raising her daughter. "You seriously do look good, Nat. Kind of lit up."

*Was that what she was?* Just the thought seemed to set off that sound in her ears. Like a steam train coming closer, or moving away, she couldn't tell which. But it was whistling. "Actually, you do, too, Mom."

"Yeah, well. Nice moon."

"It's not the moon." Natalie meant it, but was still surprised when her mother nodded.

"It's the babies. Yours. Soph's. Being alone with them all last night and most of today, since Soph didn't come by either until maybe an hour ago, and I had to call in sick to work."

"Sorry. Don't snark."

"Did that sound snarky?"

"Don't be sad. We're okay. We're all—"

"Do I look sad?"

Natalie looked. "Not tonight, actually."

Jess nodded. "See?"

Shaking her head, still dazed, Natalie started out the door. The early summer air swirled around her, heavy and warm.

"At least take the car," her mother called when she was already across the square of dirt that constituted their yard.

"I'd rather walk," Natalie said.

"Cars are for driving. For getting you places."

"Not to Waffle House. Not that car."

"Oh, brother."

"'Night, Mr. Rogers."

When Natalie heard no laughter, she glanced back. Jess leaned in the doorway of the trailer, arms folded, head against the frame. Natalie had the disconcerting impression that the trailer was moving slowly away like a boxcar hitched to an invisible engine. Then the feeling passed, and the night sucked her out into it.

All the way up Sardis Road, she had to resist the urge to cover her ears. The cicadas were deafening, their sawing seeming to emanate not just out of the ground but from the trees, the power lines, her own eyes and ears, as though she herself were producing it. To escape, she forwent her traditional pause-and-whimper in the drainage ditch across the street from the Waffle House and just stalked straight across the parking lot, gave the finger to the Wheel-of-Fortune letters that made up the sign, and pushed inside.

"*Damn*, Nat," her boss, Benny, said when she was halfway around the counter, her waitress apron already off its peg and settling on her shoulders. She turned, met his stare, dropped a hand to her hip.

"What? I'm three seconds late and you're going to complain?

Seriously?"

Instead of answering, he stared some more. If anything, he looked even more bristly than usual, wiry white-gray hair sticking straight up off his scalp, out from his lip, seemingly poking holes in the collar of his apron. He stood maybe 5'3", a couple inches taller than Natalie's mother. *World's friendliest walking toilet brush*, Sophie called him. Affectionately. Accurately. Natalie felt a stab of something in her chest, for no good reason, and swayed on her feet.

"You do something with your hair?" Hewitt asked, moving past Benny out of the kitchen with five plates of French fries on his arms and that smile on his lips that had cost her so dearly. Blessed her forever.

Natalie rolled her eyes. "Like you'd notice."

"Just did." He bumped her with his hip as he rolled by.

*And there he goes*, Natalie thought. *The father of my child.* Dealing out French-fry plates, refilling ketchup canisters with a graceful sweep of his arm. Tall and tan and gristle-bearded and grinning, as ever. The grin never overbearing, always hungry to find its reflection on another's face. It had looked so welcoming, so impossibly sexy and bright at camp that summer, when Natalie was twelve and he was nineteen. It had looked even sexier four years later, the night she came across him and his laughing, goofball friends bowling backwards and between their legs at the basement alley on Independence, and surprised him by flouncing down and demanding that he remember her. Then she'd lunged in and kissed him before grabbing Sophie's hand and racing away, screaming and laughing. It had still looked sexy, if a little pathetic, last summer, three weeks after she started at Waffle House and found him waiting tables there. After which she'd finally lured him out for a night and fulfilled a silly, decade-old fantasy and started paying the price for it.

It even looked a little sexy now, she thought, on the face of an exhausted 31-year-old Waffle House waiter with little ambition except to avoid as much of what came next as possible, little or nothing of interest to say, and no ill will toward anyone he'd ever met. Which made that smile real, all right, but inhuman, somehow. Stitched in place. A scarecrow's grin. Which hadn't scared her enough.

"Hey, seriously," Benny said behind her. "*Is* it your hair?"

"Um. Did I wash it, you mean?" For Benny, though, Natalie mustered a tired smile of her own. Because he actually would have noticed, did seem to care. And because he had Rose Maddox on his jukebox, going honky tonkin'. The whole room seemed to bob under Natalie's feet.

Benny stopped staring at her face long enough to eye the rest of her. His gaze was usually father-like, not lecherous, but tonight it disturbed her, for some reason, and the fact that it did made her heart ache.

"Can I get some syrup that's actually warm here?" called the trucker at the end of the counter. Only when Natalie brought him some did she realize that that guy was staring at her, too. The syrup he already had felt plenty warm when Natalie collected the bottle from his table.

And so it went, all night long. Even the jukebox seemed under her spell. Not a single person hit the Metallica button or called up "We're an American Band." Instead, they all selected the songs she loved, wailin' Roy and Howlin' Wolf, the King, and Kitty, the whole column of tracks Bertie had threatened to replace with Mariah Carey singles until Natalie told him that if he did, she'd quit and also key his Lincoln. Inevitably, some staggering teen in an *I MADE IT ON MYRTLE BEACH* T-shirt summoned "Sweet Home Alabama," but even that sounded strangely perfect, primal, the way it sometimes did when no one slurred along to it—or everyone did—and that riff rolled the whole room onto its shoulders and lit out for the low country. Every time she passed the trucker who'd asked for warmer syrup, and who couldn't seem to get himself off his stool and leave, he'd order more coffee and then stare openly at Natalie's ass as she walked away. But he made no grab for it, never once looked like he'd even thought of it, and somehow, he just seemed hopeless there, like he'd forgotten where he was or what clocks or forks were for. Every time she passed the inevitable half-drunk teens in their booths, they'd go quiet, lean together, some of them smiling at her, not a one puking into his or her fries. A whole family came in—a nighttime rarity for Waffle House—looking exhausted from driving too long. The father gave Natalie a too-friendly smile, but the mom did, too, and the kids leaned against their parents and the orange plastic backs of their booths and slept. Bertie tossed Natalie plates so fast and smoothly over the kitchen transom that he seemed to be juggling.

Every time the front door opened, Natalie could hear cicadas, even above the music, or she thought so, anyway, a siren call she couldn't quite drown out but didn't need to heed, not yet. Meanwhile, all night, the air flowed in, summer-sweet and pear-scented and warm.

All of this was hers, Natalie thought at one point, moving in endless, automatic circles through the room. These smells and these people leaning together and going quiet when she passed, because their conversations had inevitably circled way too close to things people couldn't normally say to each other, or had meant to say years ago, the way conversations tend to in chain diners under fluorescent light in the middle of the night.

Sophie appeared around one-thirty, her baby sleeping in a sling against her breasts, her face scrubbed clean, cheeks bright, kinked blond hair wet and loose and cascading over her child like a bead curtain. The warm-syrup trucker twitched on his stool, glanced away from Natalie for once, and seemed to fold even deeper into himself with his eyes wide and his mouth turned down.

"What's with the bullfrog?" Sophie said upon approaching the counter, jerking her chin toward the trucker. Voice sparkling, arm supporting her child, smile wide. As if she were still just Sophie, and last night had never happened.

Natalie shrugged. "He appears to be a little lost."

"Or hungry. Those are some bulgy eyes he's got. Watch out, passing flies."

For once—no, as usual—Sophie's chirping grated on Natalie. In a good way. Somehow, she felt that more of this particular night should have irritated her than it had so far.

"Shouldn't you be asleep, Sophie? Or home watching your son sleep? You want eggs?"

Sophie swung around, caught the eye of the father in the booth, sipping coffee while his kid slept in his lap. Then she turned back, looking surprised. "Um. Nah. I don't know. Later. Not hungry."

Natalie realized she wasn't, either. Despite having slept the entire day. And worked fast for hours. She hadn't even had a sip of coffee.

*Or water? Was that right?*

Sophie drummed the countertop, bobbed up and down on the balls of her feet, did it again. "I feel like Kanga," she said. Gazed down into the sling. "With my Roo." Which is what she mostly called her son. She looked up. "Only sexier."

The tears ambushed Natalie so fast, just appeared on her face, she felt as though she'd walked through a spider web. *What was she crying for?* So many things: the trailer; her son's bassinet wedged between the fold-down table and the sink; her mother the lawn gnome; these people moored in this nowhere place on the outskirts of this 200-year-old void of a city like lost boats at a buoy in the middle of the ocean; that sawing in her ears; her best and oldest friend's face, so bright, so familiar, hovering over her son, smiling and aggravating and beautiful as ever. She let the tears come, put a hand to her heart.

**35**

And that's when she knew. Understood almost everything, even before she glanced over Sophie's shoulder out the window and saw the black Sierra in the lot, parked lengthwise across the handicapped spots right in front of the door. The squat African American woman standing with her arms folded beside the open door of the cab, and beside her, the Whistler, all knees and elbows with his workshirt untucked and his chin on his chest and that sombrero over his face so that only his bottom lip was visible. His stance made him look heeled, obedient, like some scrawny Blackmouth Cur.

Natalie went still, tingling. Her tears damming themselves, now, as the shutters dropped down behind her eyes. Her mother had taught her this trick. Or instilled it, by osmosis. She was amazed to find it still worked. Wiping once at her face, she drew her apron over her head. They all noticed, everyone in the restaurant except Sophie, because they were all watching. Natalie started past her friend for the door. Her body seemed to settle, steel itself under her skin. Her shoulders drew back.

The father in the booth was the one who finally went past staring, wolf-whistled and grabbed right up under her skirt as she passed. Natalie broke his nose with one savage, sideways punch. So easy, like smashing a Frosted Mini-Wheat. The secret—as she'd learn later—turned out not to be any newfound strength or power, but the spell she cast. The way the sight of her gripped people, got in their muscles and synapses, prevented them from defending or even reacting.

As she pushed out into the night, she realized she even knew what the whistling in her ears was. Not cicadas. Not power lines. Not the echo of the Whistler's breath in her ears. Just the sound the world makes rushing through a pipe, or pooling in a cistern. Whipping through a dead place, with neither heartbeat nor bloodrush to impede it.

"He's got something to tell you," the squat woman said before Natalie had even reached them, and then she climbed into the cab and shut the door.

The Whistler didn't look at her right away. He kicked at an invisible pebble, the gesture studied and too slow, like he thought he was in a car-hop scene from *American Graffiti*. As if he might ask her to go steady. His mouth pursed even more than last night, and his dark eyes wide, as though he were nervous, full of regret. And something else. Only much later, with a gurgle of disbelief, did Natalie recognize it as hope.

She stared for a while at those eyes, passed a cursory glance over his mouth. It exerted no pull, tonight. It wouldn't, she thought, even if he whistled. *Because she was no longer capable of being pulled*? A tremble rippled through her, and the tears rose again, and Natalie battled them back.

"Go on," she said. "Say what you're going to."

"I'm sorry," said the Whistler, sounding plenty sincere. And then he told her. Then the squat woman got out, shoved him back in the cab of the truck, and told her some more.

When they were done, and the Sierra had gone, Natalie let herself stand still in the empty lot for one long moment. The light behind her almost warm on her back. And nothing else warm, anywhere.

Eventually, she reentered the Waffle House, balling her apron and dropping it to the floor like shed skin. "Benny," she called over the jukebox racket and the rumble of ordinary, hopeless, everyday conversation, "I quit. Sorry." As she passed the booth with the family, Jerry Lee urged her to grab the bull by the horns. So she grabbed Sophie by the shirt collar and yanked her off the father whose nose Natalie had broken.

"What?" Sophie chirped. "I was cleaning him up."

"By climbing him?"

"You broke his nose."

"You were suffocating him," Natalie said, nodding toward the smear of blood across the rim of Sophie's cleavage. Her Roo had shifted around to her back, still somehow sleeping through it all. The father, dazed, tipped sideways onto the shoulder of his own son. His wife sat blank across the table, staring at her husband in astonishment, not sympathy. Certainly not understanding.

*Not his fault*, Natalie wanted to tell her. Tingling again. That whistling, that would never stop, ever, threatening to drown out every other sound. *Not my fault, either.*

She dragged Sophie out the door into the dark. "Hurry up," she said, climbing into the passenger seat of the Kia and beating repeatedly on the French fry-greased dashboard until Sophie finished locking her son into his seat.

"What's your *damage*?" Sophie snapped. But she knew Natalie better than to wait. She dropped the car in gear and drove them back to

Honeycomb Corner.

"Don't move," Natalie snapped when they'd pulled up in front of her mother's dark trailer. She got out, stalked around the Kia, opened the backseat door, and had Roo out of his straps before Sophie realized what was happening.

"What the fuck are you doing?"

Natalie whirled. Sophie's son squirming once in his blanket in her arms. Little coil of heat. "Say goodbye," Natalie said.

Sophie blinked. Stared. Started to get out.

"Stay *there*," Natalie hissed.

Sophie hesitated, half-in half-out of the Kia. Tears finally rising in her eyes, too. "Nat?" she said. So small.

Inside, Natalie laid the boy next to Eddie in the bassinet. Both of them squirming now, settling into each other. Wolf-pups in a den. *While their moms go hunting*, she thought, snarled the thought down, went into her mother's room, dropped her hands on either side of her mother and woke her up.

"Don't say anything," she said, staring hard down into Jess' still, silent face. The eyes already open, sharp, quiet. She just lay there, in that stupid flowered bathing cap she always wore to sleep in, because she said she hated her hair tickling. "Mom. Just listen."

Her mother stared back. Not scared. Not anything she was going to reveal yet. Still and always the single smartest living thing Natalie had ever known.

"Get out of Charlotte," Natalie said. "Tomorrow. Take them both. Eddie and Roo. Leave no trace. Do you understand? No trace."

No reaction.

"Mom. Are you listening?"

Stupid question. She'd never once stopped listening, all Natalie's life.

"I'm sorry," Natalie said, let the shutters behind her eyes crack open just once, then slammed them shut again. "No trace. I'm not planning to come looking. But whatever you do…don't let me find you."

Sophie was out of the car when Natalie emerged from the trailer. The empty sling hung like a burst cocoon from her shoulders. She was crying, but not asking. Starting to know. Natalie moved toward her, stopped in the dirt, under the crescent moon, and stared at the Kia. Then she glanced toward the edge of the lot, where the dark-chocolate GTO she'd spent five years saving for and two rebuilding sat against the fence, like a stallion in its paddock, just waiting.

"Come on," Natalie said. "We're taking *my* car."

## Two Thousand Miles
## I Roamed

*He made sure, the next night, while Mother drove due south down the 55 and wouldn't stop and wouldn't even turn on the radio, to stay curled against the door, sombrero tilted down, arms wrapped tight to himself. Poor little tomcat. That was him.*

*"Why would you do that?" she kept asking, and he kept not answering, tucking his chin down tighter so she couldn't see his face. "Why? All these years and years—how many years?—and you've never once done it."*

*"Never even tried," he murmured.*

*"I didn't even know you knew how."*

*"I didn't."*

*He could feel her stare through the tilted-down hat-brim, and from somewhere way down in the oldest nuclei of his oldest cells, he felt a delicious, discomforting flicker. Not fear of her. But* memory *of fear of her. From the years right after she'd found him.*

"Then how?"

He shrugged. Yawned. "I think I just…wanted to."

A jerk of the wheel, a spatter of gravel and pebbles, and the truck ground to a stop on a lightless stretch of shoulder. Flat, empty highway in both directions. Tobacco fields to either side, their wrinkled leaves lolling like dry tongues, stretching for the moonlight. Cicadas whistling.

"Why?" Mother said again.

He looked up, then. Let her see his face. "Because she's my Destiny," he said, and watched her draw back. Enjoyed that.

"I am your destiny. I've kept you safe, all these years. And well fed."

"I think…" the Whistler said, and pursed his lips to whistle, and decided that was rude. Unnecessarily cruel. Maybe just a bit dangerous, which made him want to start again. But he didn't. "I think I have been yours. Isn't that right, Mother?"

Instead of answering, Mother drew herself up. Still so lithe when she rose like that. Beautiful black mamba. So fast. Taller, suddenly, than even he expected, and he knew every inch of her, every gesture. "And if you're right?" she purred. "What do you imagine that changes?"

He didn't answer. Wasn't ready to, not quite yet. So he gazed out across the fields, feeling the pull of his Destiny. Relishing that. Thinking of her eyes staring up at him as he fed on her, reached for her, across the moat of her own blood. So nearly his, she was. Though not quite yet. "It's what you imagine that's going to matter," he said. "That's going to be the determiner. Don't you think?"

"Eighty years," Mother hissed. "Eighty years. I'd call that destiny. Both of ours. Wouldn't you? In fact, we've been all sorts of people's destinies. You and me."

"Sure," he said. "Like cancer."

"Like a car crash," Mother agreed, right in rhythm, reciting the catechism she'd taught him. Choose at random. Disappear.

"Except cancers don't choose at all, Mother. And they don't have Destinies."

"They also—"

"And they can't fall in love," he said.

Mother couldn't have choked to more satisfying silence if he'd thrown his hands around her neck and wrung her. From down in his lungs, in the dead reservoir under his heart, he could feel his whistle rising again.

"Love," Mother said, as though pushing out a peach pit. Then, with more force, "Love!"

"You haven't been with her," he said. "You don't know her."

"I know you." And then—for the first time in so very long—she surprised him. Reached across and touched his shoulder. Then his face. "We've gotten along. We really have."

"Mother. This has nothing to do with you. It's love."

"All this roaming we've done."

Two thousand miles we roamed. Just to make this truck our home. He hummed in his head all the way to the whistling part. The greatest whistling part—the whistle of the singer's own death coming, three days after he recorded it—but he stopped his lips from pursing, for just a little longer. Like a lover, *teasing the song. Teasing himself. Such total, exquisite agony. He turned, and he and Mother looked at each other. Not-mother, not-son.*

*"Looks like nothing's going to change," he said.*

*"Stop it."*

*"Can't do what my Mother tells me to do."*

*"You really think you can have love, and still eat? You think you even remember what love feels like, assuming you ever felt it?"*

*So badly, the Whistler wanted to whistle. To call his Destiny to him. Instead, he shrugged. "They eat." He gestured out the window into the world they'd roamed.*

*Abruptly, Mother's face twisted into its snakey smile. "So if you love her… why did you lie to her?"*

*The question caught him off-guard. He hadn't even realized she'd listened when he talked to his Destiny, though of course she would have. He'd been too hypnotized by his Destiny's face to care. Her furious but tearless eyes in the yellow Waffle House light. Dark, sweat-damped hair on her neck, and the night threading through her, knitting her to it.*

*"Why?" Mother pressed, sensing, unerringly, his momentary weakness. "Why not tell her what's really going to happen? If you love her. If you're planning to travel together. Forever."*

*For just a moment, the Whistler forgot music. Forgot his Hunger, which was all but overpowering, now, because he hadn't eaten enough, hadn't been able to, not if he wanted to save his Destiny. Forgot the rules of the game every conversation with Mother became, catch-and-parry. He simply considered the question she'd asked.*

*Eventually, he sighed. "I'm not completely sure. Instinct, I think. She's… strong, my Destiny. Stubborn. Better to let her fend for herself, for a little while. Discover for herself. That way —"*

*"Destiny," Mother snorted. "Is that why you changed her friend, too? The little blonde?"*

*Now, the Whistler did smile. And he finally let out the first long, piercing whistle of the night. She'd had him off balance for a second. Uncertain. Until she'd accidentally reminded him of exactly how strong his love for his Destiny was.*

*How strong his love was.*

*"The blonde is to keep her company," he said, silencing Mother yet again. "For a little while. So that she's not lonely. Or else the energy just spilled over. Or maybe it was my Destiny's Need. You have no idea how strong she is, Mother. The day will come when she knows, when she's ready. And sooner than you think. Sooner than you think."*

*Once more, Mother snake-swayed in her seat. Watched, while he sat, whistling. Two cobras, their dance instinctive, automatic. Mating, killing, same difference.*

*"What if she doesn't Finish?" she said. The Whistler didn't answer, and she leaned forward. Smiling, all teeth. "What if she won't? She's strong, your Destiny. You said it yourself." When he still didn't answer, she let her smile slip. "Are you Hungry?"*

*And right at that moment, the way it happened sometimes — surprisingly often, almost often enough to convince him that he and Mother's life really did follow a trajectory, a logic if not a Destiny — two hitchhikers appeared in the* truck's headlight beams. The first was a prickle-faced, sandy-haired youth, maybe twenty-five, with a suitcase in one hand and the other in his coat pocket, curled around whatever he had that he thought was going to protect him. The girl beside him looked much younger. Too young, really. When they could, he and Mother generally avoided the young ones.

Poor little girl. Hair like frayed yellow yarn, eyes glassy in the headlights, dead as headlights. The Whistler sat up straight. Whistled, long and sad, while the prickle-faced youth stepped cautiously around the hood of the truck, hand coming out of his pocket to lock like a handcuff around the girl's resistance-less wrist.

I will liberate you first, *he thought, watching the girl.* I will sing you to sleep.

"Will she do?" Mother asked, softly.

"Oh, yes," the Whistler breathed.

*In response, Mother gunned the engine and sent the truck hurtling past the diving hitchhikers and down the highway. And in spite of himself, the Whistler twisted around, looked back to watch them recede, vanish in the thin night mist.*

*Beside him, Mother let out a low, humorless laugh. But she didn't turn, the Whistler noticed. Wouldn't quite look at him. Which meant that she knew—though she wouldn't admit it, not yet—that she should probably be afraid.*

*Smiling, the Whistler settled back in the passenger seat, tucked his arms against the Hunger-knot in his guts, closed his eyes, conjured up his Destiny's face. And hummed.*

## Help Me, Information

"You know," Sophie called out the car window toward where Natalie stood just off the highway shoulder, "this was more fun when it was a challenge." Then she pushed the red-haired guy's head back down between her legs. "That's it," she told him, patting him, leaning her own head back. "Good dog."

Instead of answering, Natalie stepped through the curtain of Spanish moss hanging off the roadside oaks into the forest. It really was like stepping through a waterfall into a fairyland, the moss as much *de*flecting as reflecting the moonlight, turning everything into its own negative. She spread out her arms, imagined the moss draping her, too, transforming her into a Natalie-shaped shadow.

"Ooh, not that I'm complaining," Sophie cooed.

*Eddie*, Natalie thought, closed her eyes, kept her arms outstretched, resisted the urge to fold them into herself. She wanted to feel the full force of the emptiness there, where her child had been. To know it was permanent. She *needed* to know that, if she hoped to go on. If she did.

"Hurry up," she called back, after a while.

"Well, okay, hang on," Sophie said. "Have to thank my new friend here."

Which wasn't a Sophie-ism, Natalie knew. Not yet. For tonight— still—Sophie meant only that she was going to send her evening's toy home ravished and grateful. And living.

A short time later, Sophie joined her in the clearing. For a while, they didn't speak. Sophie settled on her rumpled skirt in the pine needles and dirt, and the cicadas sang, not to them but around them. Only the moon moved, very slowly. And the moss. Lazily. Imperceptibly, except to the trees. A kinder vampire than the one they'd met. Not that the Whistler had been unkind, really. Except for killing them.

"Do you think light screams when you drink it?" Sophie asked, and Natalie was startled by how closely even their thoughts now ran together.

"When the trees drink it, you mean?"

"Whoever." With a flourish, Sophie finished etching her name, in cursive, in the forest floor with a stick.

Natalie watched her friend lean back, catch the moonlight on her neck and roll it down into her blouse, fold her legs up to her chest. "Sophie, did that..." she started, and felt almost shy for a second before realizing how ridiculous that was. "Does it still feel good to you? The guys, I mean."

Now Sophie looked startled, almost guilty. After a moment, she shrugged."It feels warm."

"Yeah," Natalie said.

"Especially their mouths."

Which was exactly right. Mostly, these last few nights, Natalie found herself hovering around their lips, in the same way she'd once crouched beside the tiny space heater her mother used, on surprisingly frigid Charlotte winter nights, to heat the trailer. That, apparently, was what sex would be about from now on. The ghost of tingling. Mostly heat.

"Upside-down cake," Sophie said.

Natalie felt herself smile, gratefully. "What?" she barked.

"Your dad."

Natalie stopped smiling. "What are you talking about?"

"Remember your dad, when he told you he was dying? When we were like nine?"

Lowering to her haunches helped Natalie keep from lunging. And also got her in position to do so more effectively. "Strangely enough, I do."

"How you walked into his hospital room like two hours after they'd told him he had however many months to live, and he was sitting up in bed eating an entire pineapple upside-down cake?"

Abruptly, Natalie understood. The coiling in her legs loosened, and her shoulders relaxed.

"You always said he looked so happy," Sophie said.

It was true. And had stayed true for weeks. He'd eaten half a cake a day, bought himself a 25-foot headphone extension cord and rocked around their little rented house all night while his wife and daughter slept, blasting "Paralyzed" and "Time Has Come Today" into his brain. "Audio morphine," he'd said over bowls of Super Sugar Crisp every morning, grinning. That had continued until the cake and the Crisp stopped tasting good, started coming back up. Until the music itself sickened him with longing for things he wasn't going to be around to hear or feel, things he'd never help his daughter learn to hear or feel.

Was that what this past two weeks had been? Hers and Sophie's pineapple upside-down days?

"You know what he said he was happiest about?" Natalie murmured, putting her cold hand to the warm earth, which would never be warm enough.

"Seeing my grinning, gorgeous face at your side every day?"

Natalie closed her eyes. "He said he'd lived his whole life scared of what was going to get him. Ever since he was a little kid. He wasn't ever afraid of being dead, just how he was going to get there."

When she opened her eyes, Sophie was crouching over her scrawled name, staring down into it as though reading tea leaves. "Know what's going to get us, Nat?" Her sudden grin dazzled in that dim place, as though she'd dragged the moon right down into the clearing with them. "*Nothing*! *Ever*!" Then she leapt to her feet and whooped.

She waited until they were back in the car, with the engine running, before she said, "Let's call home. Let's call the kids."

Until that second, for the first time in days, Natalie had started to feel pretty good. Like she really *had* had a past. A mom and dad and home and memory. Like she really was still someone, even if she wasn't who she'd been. But now the feeling fell away, like a fallen leaf she'd tried tacking to a dead branch. "No," she said.

"Come on." Sophie turned in her seat, started to touch Natalie's hand but decided not to. "Come on. I miss my Roo."

"No."

"Natalie, don't you want to hear Eddie's—"

"No," Natalie growled, and felt something, all right, a needle prick where her heart had been. Or still was. And there it came again.

"I can't stand it."

"Me either."

"Let's call. I didn't say go there. Just call."

"No."

"Natalie—"

Her hand hit the horn so hard that she left a dent in the steering wheel. The blare shredded the forest silence and even overwhelmed the whistling in her ears, just for a moment. When she finally let up, both she and Sophie stared at the dent. Then they glanced at each other.

"So…" Sophie said after a while. "You're saying no. Have I got that right?"

Out of habit, Natalie pushed air out of her mouth. It was more like blowing bubbles in a pool than breathing, but still sort of satisfying. "We couldn't, anyway. Remember? They're gone." *At least,* she thought, *they'd better be. If you listened, Mom. If you saw.*

They sat some more. In her ears, the whistling settled back into its permanent groove in her skull, a cricket hum that accompanied her everywhere, now. The only way she knew she was awake.

"So no calling," Sophie said again. And then, when Natalie looked up, "How about bowling?"

Which is what they did, and that felt fine, for a while. They found lanes on the outskirts of suburban Savannah open for midnight bowling, which proved crowded and dark and loud and buzzing. The snack bar served mustardy barbecue, not microwave pizza, and the meat smelled marvelous, wet and sweet, though neither Sophie nor Natalie could quite get a piece in their mouths. The stereo blasted mostly dirty-South hip-hop, Outkast and the Goodie Mob, but the throb felt great, juddering up through the floorboards and vibrating every-body, providing a pretty fair simulation of circulation, of actual feeling. And that, Natalie realized now, staring down the rows of trapped teenagers, bored and drunk sorority girls, was what this music—maybe all music—was always meant to do. Rattle bone-cages. Wake the dead.

They bowled three full games, the conversation and laughter and come-on all around them sweeping them up, carrying them with it like driftwood in a river current. Between turns, they kept to the shadowed benches, away from the light, and mostly, no one seemed to notice them. At least, that's what Natalie thought, and it felt right, wonderfully meaningless, eventless, endless, ordinary, until she went to the bathroom to wash her face.

She didn't even hear the kid come in. She stood at the mirror a while, staring into the blackness in her own eyes, trying to decide if she was relieved that she could still see them. That was one myth dispensed, anyway. *But were those really her eyes? Those black, blank pools? Was it worse if they had changed, or if they hadn't?*

She turned around, and there he was. Fourteen years old, maybe? Twelve? Little blond Calvin spikes, Korn T-shirt, blue eyes wide, mouth agape. Front of his shorts so distended he looked like he was about to be lifted away, Lorax-style, only from the front. Lower lip quivering. And—good god—tears in his eyes. He was blocking the door.

"You're so..." he gurgled.

"I know," Natalie sighed. "Could you move?"

"...beautiful," he finished. And then he fell to his knees.

In the end, she had to shake him off her leg like a dog, bang him a little harder than she intended—or, at least, than she seemed able to control—against the doorframe. His arms slackened and he slid down the wall, whimpering. Not in pain. Not yet. But because she was leaving. She grabbed Sophie off her bench, and they fled.

Some indeterminate, silent stretch of hours later, another hundred miles down the forested, unlit back roads along the Georgia coast,

Natalie stopped at a gas station. Her GTO, purring with use, thrummed as she shut it down. She didn't get out right away, just sat behind the wheel. Over the tops of the pine trees, the first little knick of pink appeared. Red and dripping little papercut in the dark.

"It'll be light soon," Sophie murmured, sounding less content than usual. She'd also stayed quiet longer than usual.

"I know," said Natalie. "Next hotel we see." She propped her door open. "I'm going inside for a sec. Want anything?"

"Like who?"

Half out of the car, Natalie turned. "That's not funny."

But Sophie wasn't grinning. Not all the way. Her voice stayed small, and scared them both. "I wasn't entirely kidding, I don't think."

"Then shut up."

Slamming the door, Natalie jammed the nearest pump into the gas tank and stalked off toward the station. She hadn't really thought of what she'd do in there. She just wanted…one more sight of someone, maybe. Anyone, really. And not like Sophie had meant. Surely, not. Not yet. *Please.*

The mini-mart was lit up, but locked, and Natalie had turned to go back to the car when she heard the voice from around the corner of the building. It was pleading, too.

"I'm sorry," it was saying. Slurring. "Baby. Come on. I'm so tired. Just…the lawn. Let me sleep on the lawn. Baby." Then came the wet, gargling, throat-clearing. "Love ya. You know. Baby."

Like a moth—no, dragonfly—drawn to the vibration, Natalie felt herself turn, start around the corner. There he was, splayed against the side of the building like a felled bowling pin. He wore a rumpled three-piece suit, black shoes that still shone, and had gristly stubble along his neck, at which Natalie just kept staring. His Adam's apple bobbed up and down like bait on the surface of a river.

"I know I've promised before," he was whining, starting to sob into the cell phone at his ear, in a way that suggested that the person on the other end had already hung up. Might have done so long ago. "Come on, you know you're the only…"

He looked up and saw Natalie. Apologies continued to spill from him, as if from a vein he'd opened. But the cell phone slipped out of his hands.

"Oh, come on, really?" Natalie snapped, hands on her hips, as the guy on the ground started to blubber, just like the kid in the bowling alley bathroom. "You're all going to cry now?"

"I'm sorry." His voice was high, thin as a midge's whine. "I can't help…I'll stay. I'll…do anything…" And he reached out his arms. As though he wanted to be tucked in.

In two long strides, Natalie was over him, dropping down on top of him. She was thinking—hoping, maybe—he'd be too drunk too respond, but he wasn't. Or she was just too much. Under her skirt, through his pants, she felt him stiffen. Felt the warm asphalt on her bare, cold legs. The moonlight on her back. The night, her ocean, swirling around her.

His eyes overflowed as he stared up at her. In gratitude, she thought with amazement, and also disgust, and something else she didn't even want to think about. At least the sight kept her own gaze away from his throat.

And the longer she looked at him, the more he relaxed. Stiffened, and relaxed. Opening himself to her. Practically begging. Ridiculous silver stud in one of his ears. And—even more ridiculous—a pencil behind the other ear.

She felt herself bend forward. Toward his mouth, not his neck. Staring at him the whole time. Holding him fast. It was just so easy. Which made her so sad. Her lips like ice-cubes, melting against his. Turning liquid once more. Almost human. So soft. She hardly pressed. He pressed, but only to keep the contact, to extend it. Because he could sense that's what *she* wanted. Because she could communicate that, now, without even trying, the way she never had been able to when it had mattered. The way no one apparently could. Not really. Not while they were living. Not to anyone else living.

He was flat-out weeping, now, still kissing her. So warm. She lifted herself up, just an inch. Stared into him. Saw him in there, little and scared, though not scared enough. Chuck Berry in her ears, over the whistling. Calling his little Marie, in Memphis, Tennessee. Little Eddie in her heart, the ghost of his weight in her arms. Never to rest there again.

Her grip tightened on the arms underneath hers. She stared at the

Adam's apple, at this pathetic guy's furiously blinking eyes, willing them to stillness. They stilled. She kissed him once more.

"There," she said. "You've had what you were looking for, now. There's nothing else. I promise. And I should know. Go home."

She stood up. He lay frozen. On impulse, without any clear reason, she bent again and took his cell phone. Then she started back toward her car.

She'd been around more than enough guns in her life to recognize the click of a safety-catch when she heard it. But all she thought, as she stopped in her tracks, was, *Asshole.* If what he'd really wanted was sympathy, someone to beg him not to end his pitiful life…well, that was almost funny, come to think of it.

She'd turned to say so, and to suggest another option if dying was what he really wanted, when he shot her.

### Never Close Her Eyes and Sleep
### 'Til We Were All In Bed

For a while, she did what she'd always done: got up and got at it. And that was all right.

The second Natalie had left, she stood, threw on her skirt and sweater, fixed her only suitable blanket over both babies in the bassinet, and sang them the "Pony Man" verse about the midnight meadow and the cats in the shed. They were already sleeping, but those lines were a spell, had charmed even her buzzing beehive of a daughter into deepest dream all those years ago, and Jess needed these babies dreaming now. When they were all the way still, she hurried next door and got Wanda to sit watch in the trailer while she went for supplies.

"If Natalie shows up, don't let her in," Jess told the old woman when she'd gotten herself and her quilt and her crocheting wedged in the folding chair next to the trailer's tiny sink. "Tell her to wait right out there." On impulse, she started to pull a butcher knife out of the block to give to Wanda, then reconsidered. If Natalie had wanted the babies tonight, she could have taken them. Or not even come home.

"Aw, Jess, honey, what's she gone and done?"

"Nothing she's going to finish." For one moment, as the snarl left her mouth, the enormity of that statement dropped on her. She saw her daughter's face, the way it had looked less than an hour before, hovering over her. *Get out of Charlotte,* she'd said. *Don't let me find you.* Hands holding Jess down in the sheets as though drowning her, eyes black and panicked and lost and hard.

The hardness had made Jess just a little bit proud. That was perverse, of course. But it helped her shove everything else she thought she'd seen out of her mind, at least for the moment.

"It can't be that bad," Wanda yawned, sagging against the back of the chair, wrinkly eyelids drooping. "You of all people know that."

"*Get up,*" Jess snapped. Her command shot through the old woman like a defibrillator charge and straightened her. "Watch those babies. Watch that door. Please. I'm going to the pharmacy."

Wanda didn't answer, and her eyelids didn't droop. She didn't even lift the crochet from her lap.

"Thanks," Jess said. The salute Wanda snapped off almost made her smile, just for one moment, as she grabbed her keys and hurried into the night.

At the Walgreens, she bought a case of formula, all the Gerber jars on the shelf—except winter beef and pears, because no matter how desperate the situation, no grandchild or friend of her grandchild would be eating that—diapers, Desitin, Orajel, wipes, powder, and two car-seats. The seats were bulky and cheap, barely fit, couldn't be tethered properly, and seemed to tilt toward the back cushions like Ferris wheel wells. But they'd do. At home, she saw Wanda back to her own trailer, then packed the very little she'd need for herself: one suitcase of clothes, the four photo albums, the framed picture of her and Joe swinging nine-year-old Natalie between them, knee-deep in Lake Jocassee, the weekend before Joe found out just how sick he really was. The last thing she brought to the car was her satellite radio boombox, which she'd have to figure out how to plug into the lighter, because she was good and goddamned if she was going on the lam without the Orioles.

The second she heard Wanda stirring again, she stepped across the dirt between their trailers, knocked, and demanded Wanda's daughter's phone number. From Wanda's daughter, she got the name of Wanda's daughter's husband's cousin, who sold real estate in the area. Jess was almost certain she'd never mentioned him to Natalie, because why on Earth would she have?

He said he didn't deal in trailers.

"You're dealing in this one," Jess said, and there was just enough of a pause on the other end of the line to make her wonder if she'd lost her touch.

Then the cousin cleared his throat. "I guess I am," he said.

"Thattaboy." Jess told him she'd be in contact sooner or later, hung up, and dumped her cell phone in the trash.

She got the babies powdered, diapered, fed, and loaded in the car before they even seemed to realize they were awake, certainly before they started making any fuss. Not until she was pulling out of Honeycomb Corner did she glance in the rearview mirror at the metal box where she'd lived since her husband's death. The entire time she'd been a widow, every single day of her single motherhood, and the worst fourteen-year stretch in the history of the Baltimore Orioles.

Home, in other words.

How easily it comes away, she thought. A matter of hours, a handful of phone calls. Like uncoupling from a camper hookup, a quick tug and the will to do it and you're gone, almost free, to the extent that anyone who's been alive and taken a stake in others ever gets free.

In the back, Eddie began to gurgle, not crying, just reacting to the light patterns changing on the cushion that constituted his view, and Jess almost lost the wheel. She felt Natalie's face rising under her eyelids, so that every time she blinked, she had to grind her teeth to keep from crying out. She ran the Stop sign at the corner of Sardis Road, and a trombone barrage of car horns blasted her back into herself.

Lowering her gaze to the road, she drove to the bank, hauled both babies inside with her—slings, that would be the next purchase—had her safe deposit box brought, and withdrew the envelope with the life insurance check from Joe's death. Everything else—her wedding ring with its cubic zirconium stone, the foul ball her father had caught at the Orioles' second-ever home opener in April 1955, Natalie's front baby teeth and the friend bracelet she'd made on her first day of kindergarten and given to Jess—she left where it was. She'd never be back for it. But maybe someday, if Natalie ever came to her senses…if such a thing could still happen…if she was still Natalie…

With a grunt, Jess shoved her chair back, slammed down the lid of the box, grabbed both babies off the floor where she'd laid them, cashed the check, and walked out of the bank. Against her right shoulder, Eddie began to squirm, then whimper. Against her left, Sophie's Roo gummed her sleeve. Somehow wedging both kids against the car, she keyed the door open and loaded the babies in the back. Her daughter's voice was sizzling around in her ears now like a downed powerline. Saying, "Don't let me find you."

*Well, all right, Nat. If that's what you want.*

*Nat. So full of panic. My God, what happened? Where are you?*

Both kids started screaming. Because the sun was in their eyes, Jess realized. She couldn't just stand there moping. She stood anyway, just long enough to taste this moment: the final seconds of her life in her metal box, with her daughter. The first seconds of the years to come, with no metal box, or a new one, someday, somewhere. And no daughter.

"Goddamn you," she snapped, curling her right hand into a fist and then punching it so hard into the window glass that she gasped. She wasn't even sure whom she was damning. Joe, for dying. Herself, for failing. Natalie, for...

No. She couldn't think about that. Couldn't face that. What she thought she'd seen in Natalie's eyes...what she realized really might have happened—*had* happened, even though it couldn't, not really, right? Not in this world...

Somehow, she got herself back in her seat, got her screaming fingers unclenched enough to slide around the key and fit the key in the ignition. She got the car started, navigated through the bank parking lot, murmuring, "Ssh. Ssh. Babies. Kids. Come on, guys. Hush, now. Eddie, come on, hey..."

What broke her down, finally, was the realization that she didn't even know Sophie's baby's name.

Roo. Her little Roo. That's all Jess had ever heard either Natalie or Sophie call him. That's what Jess had been instructed to call him when she baby-sat, so that her brilliant, wayward daughter and her daughter's joyful, shining, wayward best friend could have at least a little bit of young-person life, despite the choices they'd made.

"Roo," she said. And then, while the babies screamed, she pulled off onto the shoulder of Sardis Road and laid her face against the steering wheel and cried.

A little later, when she'd savaged herself to silence and pulled both kids out of their seats and held and talked to and walked them awhile, she started the car again and drove them all to the Waffle House. Parking out front, she turned, though the kids were facing the back and couldn't see her.

"This'll only take a sec," she murmured. "I'll be right back. I'll never leave you. I just can't do this alone. Not again. Not anymore."

Did she realize she was making a mistake? Dropping a single bread-crumb behind her? Later, she would tell herself that she *hadn't* realized, and that even if she had, she didn't see any other choice. Maybe she was right.

The second Benny saw her, he came out from behind the counter, just as he did every single time Jess walked through his door. "The Fujiyama Mama," he said, same as always, lifting his apron over his head and wiping his hands on it. His cheeks glowed their perpetual, burnt-clay red underneath the tufts of white-gray beard. He'd loved her, she knew, for going on ten years.

"He thinks you're Snow White," Natalie had told her once.

"And he's Dwarf #8." Sophie had added. "Bristly."

"Benny," she said, looking right at him and stopping him in his tracks. Guilt rose inside her, and surprising uncertainty, and even more surprising shyness. And loss. So much loss. *Natalie…*

"Jess?" he said.

She let the tears come, didn't even try to wipe them. "Today's the day, I'm afraid."

He blinked. Then stared.

"Last chance. Only chance. I've got to go, now. I want you to come."

Everything seemed to wink out, then. The waffle and syrup smells, the clatter, even the light. She was falling through a void, reaching out for the last solid thing in sight before she dropped away into nothing, even though doing so couldn't stop her fall, wouldn't even slow her down, would just pull Benny into the void with her.

She watched him glance over his shoulder at his kitchen. His employees. The restaurant he'd worked his entire life to own. His whole world.

Then he dropped his apron on the floor and followed her out the door into the sun.

## Lonely Frog

The blood surprised Natalie. It didn't explode out of her, and it didn't gush.  But it did spatter, as though the guy had shot into a puddle.

Sophie had erupted from the car, and she came hurtling across the blacktop but stopped a few feet from Natalie, staring at the wound just below her friend's belly button. Fascinated, Natalie undid the bottom of her blouse and pulled the tails of the shirt apart. Both of them stared.

The wound looked like petals on a red flower that had bloomed in her skin. As they watched, the petals twitched, seemed to bend in toward each other, as though closing up for the night.

"Does that hurt?" Sophie asked.

"Oh, yeah," Natalie said, and threw her head back, stretching the stomach muscles to set off new whiplashes of pain all the way up her diaphragm. Actual pain. Real feeling.

Behind them, her shooter had started to blubber again. Natalie stretched her stomach some more, stuck a careful finger down by the wound, then probed inside it. The skin parted. She could feel the edges of the opening, jagged and surprisingly stiff, like little teeth. The slippery coolness inside. The sensation was delicious. Or maybe just sensation. With a sigh, she turned around.

"Uh-oh," Sophie said. Not at all unhappily.

With her finger still probing the bullet wound, Natalie cocked her head and leveled her stare. The man quivered, and the gun fell from his fingers. His mouth opened. But Natalie stopped him from speaking. Simply by wanting him to, apparently.

"That's right," she murmured, deep and low. "What is there left to say?" In five quick strides, she was beside him again, kneeling down. The man gawped at her, eyes widening. *Because he can see*, she realized. *Because he knows what's happening. And what's about to.*

Shivers exploded through her, radiating from the wound in her gut. It was all she could do not to scream, though not from pain. Not from anguish. *We've had it all wrong. All through human history. That first shocking moment of life, the world opening before us and our mouths yawning wide with the sheer, impossible shock of just* being alive, *of needing to do something to stay that way. What other choice could we have but to throw open our mouths and scream. For joy. For* joy...

Beneath her, her shooter sagged. No—relaxed. Oh, yes, he knew. The way rabbits know, once the talons seize them. Natalie smiled. Leaned forward.

"Could you get your finger out of there?" Sophie said, gesturing toward Natalie's stomach. "It's like watching you masturbate."

An hour or so later, with the blackout curtains drawn tight on the smoke-saturated motel room they'd paid for with cash from the shooter's wallet, and with the extra blankets she'd demanded from the woman at the reception desk drawn up under her chin, Natalie tried burrowing deeper into the covers, biting on the comforter to keep from grinding her teeth. In the other bed, Sophie had put on her jacket and sweater under her own blankets, and she was still playing with the guy's gun. Twirling it by the trigger guard on her finger. Aiming it, across one forearm, at the television and whispering, "*Powwwww*."

She went on doing that for some time, until finally Natalie sat up. "You're going to shoot your eye out."

"Then you can stick your finger in there," Sophie said.

Even now, Natalie couldn't decide whether she was relieved or annoyed that Sophie had made her masturbation comment at the moment she had. Certainly, she'd broken the mood and saved the guy's life, for whatever that was worth, to him or to her. As usual, the simile had seemed just a little too apt, thanks to the wetness on her fingers and the tingles crackling through her at that precise moment. Her head full of dreams she'd dared not speak, or even admit she was having.

*But she'd had them.*

"What would you have done?" Natalie whispered. "If I'd gone ahead, I mean. If I'd…?"

Sophie stopped twirling the gun. She held it between her hands. Blew across the muzzle of it, to see if her breath could sound it. A good while passed before Natalie realized that for once—for almost the first time in their lives—her friend had no answer. Or at least, none she was going to share.

"G'night," Natalie said.

"Goodnight, Natalie," said Sophie, and snuggled down in her pillow, the gun clutched to her chin and chest like a stuffed animal.

As far as Natalie could tell, neither of them slept that day. Every time she tilted toward blankness, the complete uncoupling of self that now passed for sleep, Sophie twisted in her sheets, or sang a lullaby to the gun, or got up and tiptoed to the curtains, pretending not to know Natalie was watching her, and toyed with the frayed fringe. Nudged a toe toward the slit of sunlight on the bald, brown carpet, as though squaring herself for a dive. Outside, trucks sighed and cars honked and seagulls or maybe children swept past in wind-blown clouds of screeching that might have been laughter.

The third time Sophie went to the window, she started to sing, very quietly. *"Are you sleeping…are you sleeping…little Roo…little Roo…"*

Almost, Natalie let herself join in. Let the thought of Eddie come. The ghost of his heat. His breath on her breast as she fed him. His happy, hiccupping gurgle when he ate. Seemingly of their own volition, her arms folded into a cradle across her chest, rocked the empty air. Natalie did allow herself to do that, for a single moment.

Then she rose out of the sheets—so silently she could rise, now, like a plume of smoke—lifted her pillow, and delivered a blow to the back of Sophie's head that drove her off her feet and ribs-first into the dresser against the wall.

Much faster than Natalie expected, though she should have expected, Sophie recovered, rocketed across the room for her own pillow, leapt to her bed and began to bounce. Natalie bounced, too. They stared at each other.

"Come on," Natalie growled. But her attention was distracted, just for a moment, by the gun popping up off the pillows every time Sophie landed on the mattress, nipping around her ankles like a little rat-dog. She looked up again, but too late. Sophie was already in the air, and then she was on her.

The fight lasted only a few seconds. Long enough for Sophie to rip a long gash down Natalie's cheek while ostensibly trying to smother her with the pillow, and for Natalie to jackknife, kicking her legs up and flipping Sophie ass-over-ears to bang against the night table on her way to the floor, splintering the table and exploding the lamp next to bed.

"*Ouch*," Sophie said happily, steadying herself against the bed and grabbing at the slivers of light bulb sticking like porcupine quills out of her shoulder and upper arm.

Natalie put a hand to the scratch in her face. Stroked it once.

"You done?" she said.

"Ouch," said Sophie again. And then, "Where are we going tonight?"

70

Natalie sighed. "I just got up."

"You never slept. Any more than I did."

"You have any bright ideas?"

"Only dark ones." Sophie turned on her knees, facing Natalie. "And one bright one. Let's go home."

Natalie closed her eyes. But waiting under her lids she found not Eddie, but the man who'd shot her, right at the moment his eyes sagged and his lips relaxed as her gaze settled on his throat. "We can't, Sophie."

"I have to see him, Natalie. I miss my Roo."

"I know."

"It's different for you. You know Eddie's with his grandma. Don't get me wrong, your mom's the best mom ever. I know she'll be great to both of them, but she's not my mom, and—"

"Don't," Natalie whispered, opened her eyes, trapped Sophie's. Bored into them. "Don't. Ever. Say that. Again." She got up on her all fours, moved forward across the bed. "Ever."

For a while, they stared one another down. Until Sophie said, "Which *that*, exactly? Just so I'm clear what I can't say?"

"That it's different for me."

"Ah."

They stared some more. It surprised Natalie how long Sophie could match her, now. She'd never been able to before.

Eventually, Sophie did blink. Look at the floor. Then she stood, went into the bathroom, brushed her teeth. Stayed there awhile.

Natalie got up and touched the hole in her stomach, but it was hardly there, now. A little scar, maybe not even that. A soft place. Ghost-bruise. She began brushing glass out of the carpet.

Sophie came out fully dressed. She looked pale and round and perfect in her yellow dress, her blond hair gleaming. A pool of sunshine in the dark room.

"Sorry," Natalie said.

"Nope," Sophie chirped. The chirp sounded pretty much as it always had. "You're right. As always. How about a movie? We haven't gone to the movies yet. How about *Up*, I really meant to see that?"

So they drove the GTO back toward the coast until they came to the suburbs of Savannah. They got Slurpees they didn't drink from a 7/11, and on impulse, ten-packs of Dentyne and Juicy Fruit, and waited for the late show, when Natalie prayed they'd be the only ones in the theater, because the thought of sitting in the dark next to or, good god, *behind* somebody—somebody warm, the warmth like a beacon beating, blinking under the skin—sent shivers so powerful, so *pleasurable* through her whole body that they nearly made her sick.

Back in the GTO, she stuffed four pieces of Juicy Fruit in her mouth, and was surprised how much she enjoyed that first burst of taste. Even more than the taste, she loved the give of the gum as she ground down on it, the veneer softening instantly to her bite. Yielding. Giving up.

A few seconds later, she rolled down her window and spit the gum into the night. "Tastes like…nope, not even that. Tastes like nothing."

"I know," said Sophie. "That's why I'm trying *this*." And she held up a ball she'd concocted, an entire pack of Dentyne mashed into at least four Juicy Fruit sticks. "Want one?" And she popped the ball in her mouth.

There were indeed four other people in the movie theater when they arrived, but they sat together, way in the back, and Natalie dragged Sophie to the very front. Just once, as the lights went down, Sophie sat up in her seat, glanced over her shoulder.

"But they're so cute back there," she whispered. "Don't you think they're cute? I'm pretty sure they'd like us to come sit with them. They really like my dress, I think."

Without saying a word, Natalie locked her fingers around Sophie's wrist, pushing it down into the empty cup-holder.

"Handcuffed," Natalie said.

"You're no fun," said Sophie. But she turned back and slouched and stared up at the screen.

They didn't even make it through the credits. Natalie had worried a bit about seeing the kid onscreen. Any kid. But the sight of that old guy wandering around his empty house, amid the refuse of his happy marriage, reminded her way too much of her *mother*—and she winced and glanced sideways to see Sophie with her mouth in an O and her mouth wide open.

"Are you *crying*?" Natalie hissed.

"I thought I was," said Sophie. "Though I don't seem to be."

"Why are *you* crying?"

"I said I thought I was."

They fled together out the EXIT doors into an alley, through the alley to the GTO, and back to the relative safety, or at least clarity, of the empty highway. After a while, Sophie ripped open another pack of Dentyne, made a giant new gumwad, then mushed that into place atop the muzzle of the gun.

"New lollipop flavor," she said, holding it up. "Shotgum." And she gave the gun a pet.

Natalie said nothing. She'd decided to try not to think, but that proved easier than she was expecting; the slightest push, and every thought she'd ever had scattered like dandelion seeds, leaving just her behind the wheel. A dead stem.

A hungry dead stem.

"Did we just circle whatever city this is?" Sophie asked. "Is this still Savannah? Weren't we just here?"

"I think so, yeah."

"We could try some music. You like the music."

"I *love* the music," Natalie said, and switched on the radio. Then she groaned. "I fucking hate this song."

The Troggs, claiming love was all around. Natalie had hated this song when she was dewy-eyed and ten, and still believed in such things. Sophie reached to turn the dial, and Natalie shoved her hand aside.

"No I don't," she said, surprising herself. "Apparently, I love this song." And she started to sing it. Yell it. Sophie yelled it, too, getting the words all wrong.

"*Wind*, not *wing*," Natalie barked. "How can you write anything on the *wing*?"

"Easier than on the wind," said Sophie, grinned, stuck her gumwad on her own face like a clown nose. Natalie floored the accelerator, and they hurtled away from town into the dark.

Sometime around 3 A.M., they passed a field full of cattle, and Natalie screeched the car to a stop. They didn't get out, and the animals didn't look up. The dark seemed to shape itself around the pasture, swallowing it, distending itself, a boa constrictor with cows inside it. Very occasionally, one cow bent its head to the grass. The rest just stood. Accepting whatever had come for them. Stupid, sad creatures. So helpless. Back down the road, a light came on in a nearby farmhouse, and Natalie saw a shadow cross the window in there, then the twitching flicker of a TV. A few minutes later, the TV switched off, and the figure passed the window again, settled on a couch. Love might be all around, Natalie thought. But not as much as sleeplessness. So many people on this planet. So little sleeping.

An hour before dawn, moving more slowly now, Natalie brought the car up a rise and realized she knew where they were.

"That's St. Mary's," she said, gesturing toward the surprising little sprawl of two-story wooden buildings and bedraggled peach trees lining the route to the waterfront. "We came here once. My family did."

"Do they have diners there?" Sophie asked. "Or a Waffle House?"

"You actually want…?" Natalie started to ask, turning in her seat, and the rest of the question died on her lips. She stared at her friend. Felt her thoughts scatter once more. "Oh," she said.

"Sooner or later," Sophie whispered. "We're going to have to. Know what I mean?"

Natalie shook her head. Shook it again, harder. "I have a better idea."

Five minutes later, she'd parked the GTO in an empty lot half a block from the St. Mary's River. "Come on," she said, and got out. The wind surprised her, whipping in off the Cumberland Sound. On the power lines and in the peach trees, mourning doves cooed.

"Better!" said Sophie, hopping out behind her. "Perfect. Private. Afterward, we can camp for the day below decks in an empty boat and—"

"Shut up." Natalie stalked out onto the pier, banging her feet down on the boards to feel them rock underneath her.

That worked exactly as she'd intended. Within seconds, a stubbly, hung-over sea-bum stumbled out onto the deck of his little tour boat, greeting them with a "What the hell's the racket…" before he got his eyes all the way open and saw them. Natalie stopped, and Sophie beside her. The man somehow staggered without moving his feet, like a wind-whipped shore-tree. Then he made one more sound. A surprisingly pretty one. Gentle little whimper.

"He feels it in his fingers," Sophie hummed.

For the first time all night, Natalie let herself laugh. "He feels it in his toes."

"Do…" the man tried, and seemed surprised to find his voice still working. Nice, ripply arms and skin just starting to crack under the three-day stubble and caking of salt spray. He hadn't been doing this long, Natalie decided. A second career, after losing his wife, maybe. There was hope left for him. If there were days left for him.

Sophie glanced back toward town, the buildings and streetlights depthless in the pre-dawn gray. "There's absolutely no one watching," she said, and looked at Natalie, and shivered. From expectation. From nervousness. From regret. How did Natalie know? Because she'd always known Sophie. But more, now, because what else could Sophie be feeling?

Natalie caught her friend's eyes again. Tasted her own hunger again. And shook her head. Just once.

"No?" said Sophie.

"Not yet." Then she turned to the sea-dude. "Take us to the island. To Cumberland."

"Um. Nat?" said Sophie.

Somewhere back behind his frozen, staring eyes, good only for lapping at the sight of the women before him now, the sea-dude found a part of his brain. "Don't…don't open for business until nine."

"But you'll take us now."

"But I'll take you now."

"Or we could take *him* now," Sophie whispered. Natalie pushed her onto the boat deck.

As the sea-dude stumbled up to his driving cabin and started the engines, Sophie tugged Natalie's sleeve.

"I said no," Natalie warned.

"Yeah, and I said, 'What time is it?'" Sophie gestured overhead at the sky. The pinkness not streaking it—not yet—but seeping through. Blood under skin.

Instead of answering, Natalie pulled a tarp out of an open locker at the stern of the little cruiser, slung it over her head, held it up for Sophie to join her. Together, they huddled, the tarp whipping against them as the boat chugged down the slips toward open water and the mainland receded behind them. A sudden urge to jump ship, swim madly for land, haul herself out of the river and break straight for home almost yanked Natalie to her feet.

"Hey," Sophie said, panic surfacing suddenly in her voice. "Cumberland. I've read about Cumberland. There's no...there aren't any buildings there, Natalie. There's no shelter. There's nothing. You're taking us out there to die."

"I'm taking us out there to sleep."

"You mean die. I know you. I won't go." Sophie started to stand. It startled Natalie—terrified, and also amused her—to realize that Sophie was serious. "You can do what you want, Nat. That's the one place I won't go with you. I don't want to die."

Natalie just held her friend's wrist. Tightly. "Too late," she murmured.

And Sophie stared at her. After a surprisingly long while, when the other boats had fallen away behind them and the mainland had blurred into the shadows, she settled back down again.

"Oh, yeah," she said. "I guess that's true." And then, "You're not really taking us to die. Are you?"

"To sleep," Natalie said.

"Just sleep?"

"And think. And hear alligators bellow. Ever heard an alligator bellow? It's better…" And she stopped. Astonished. Now she *was* crying. "It's better than the Whistler's whistle."

Another long while passed before Sophie shrugged and laid her head against Natalie's shoulder, shivering in the morning chill. "Oh," she said. "Cool."

At the island, they leapt together onto the pier before the sea-dude even got his ropes uncoiled and headed at a dead run for the trees. Behind them, Natalie could hear the sea-dude calling once, the call not angry, not even surprised, but full of longing. Like birdsong. The sound almost made her turn. But then she sensed the sun, just rising off the surface of the water, spreading its great, orange wings.

"Come *on*!" Sophie shouted, laughing, now, and then they were laughing together, rocketing up the hill into the woods, which welcomed them with its prickle-arms. They crunched through the fallen needles and leaves while the shadows drew closed behind them.

The place Natalie had in mind proved easy to find, less than a mile from the boat landing, right on the main trail. There, just as she remembered, the woods cleared, and they came to the ruins of the summer mansion the Carnegies had built and then abandoned after the wedding of their daughter, in the wake of the stock market crash. In the shade of the live oaks, as sunlight slid across the grass and over the tumbles of crumbled white brick and into the algae-covered pool, Sophie and Natalie crouched, quiet, leaning together. Snorting in the foliage behind them startled Sophie, but Natalie held her still. A few moments later, three white horses, their hides bramble-scratched and flea-bitten, their hooves high and hard, stepped into the clearing, shuddered together as the light hit them, and then went still, like statues that had come to life in the night and then resumed their places for the coming day. Later, having retreated a little farther into the woods in case any other visitors came along, Sophie and Natalie saw the leaves around the nearest horse's hooves hump up, as though waves had formed there. Again, Sophie spooked, and again Natalie quieted her.

"Armadillos," she whispered.

"Aww," Sophie whispered back, and leaned forward, almost to the edge of the light. "Here little guys. Want some gum?"

Their silvery backs winked amid the leaves as a little family of them made their way across the overgrown lawn and around the other side of the roofless main hall of the mansion.

"It's like *The Wind in the Willows*," Sophie whispered.

"Yeah, but then that would make us…"

"Weasels!" said Sophie happily. "Nifty."

"We can't stay here, Sophie. People come here all the time. Day-tourists."

Way back in the oaks, where the leaves got dense again and the shadows heavy and thick, they found a gazebo with its latticed sides collapsed but its columns and domed roof intact. They curled themselves in a corner, and Natalie drew the tarp she'd stolen from the boat over both of them.

"I don't think anyone will come here, do you?" she said, feeling the tarp warming, a little. Nowhere near enough to keep either her or Sophie from shivering.

"Even if they do, they won't lift this tarp," said Sophie.

"Unless they do," said Natalie.

Sophie turned her head, grabbing Natalie's eyes. "Unless they do."

A long time later, when both of them had rolled around on the hard, cracked ground and neither of them had slept—*did they need sleep? Would it come?* The Whistler hadn't said one way or the other—Sophie propped up on her elbow.

"Natalie. We have to pick someone."

"I know, Sophie."

"We have to."

"I said I know."

"He said if we didn't, instinct would take over, right? And then we'll just do it. To whoever happens across our path. And that's not right. Is it?"

"Lie down, what if someone's coming?" Natalie murmured, through the crimping in her stomach. The tickle in her parched, dry throat that water would not ease.

"I miss my Roo," Sophie whimpered.

"Yeah."

"Natalie," said Sophie, after a pause that might have lasted hours, as her freezing fingers laced into her friend's "I'm so hungry." Then she squeezed, hard.

And Natalie squeezed back, and closed her eyes. Which were completely dry, now.

"Me, too," she said.

## Hold On.

## I'm Coming.

*He had the air in his lungs and the rhythm in his legs and his lips puckered and he was just leaning back to kiss the sky once more when he realized he was going to kill Mother. Really kill her. Tonight. Before he ate.*

*But after the set. The whistle was in his throat, roaring toward the open air, and he couldn't have stopped it if he wanted to, and he didn't want to. That first shriek shocked even him, as it often did, and he felt himself soar up behind it, straight out of his dead-leaf skin. Up and up, until it really did seem he could look down from way above the stage, straight through the too-low ceiling of this cramped little club that could never contain him, through clouds that couldn't hold him either, and see those pathetic bodies below, every one of them with their faces turned up, their hands frozen halfway to their heads as if they weren't sure whether to throw them over their ears or up in the air. As if they really believed they could block his whistle out. Even the band he'd joined for*

83

*the night seemed to fall away, still spurting noise, spent stages of the rocket he'd used to catapult himself free.*

*And then he swooped back down. Rode the rhythm right back into his rib cage, right there amongst them, so he could feel their shudders as the whistle went in. Catch their breaths in the hairs of his arms. Kneeling at the foot of the stage, he opened up a staccato gunfire burst and watched the whole front row rock back, then fall forward as he sucked them in. Every single one of them with their eyes open and on him, their mouths, too, halfway screaming, halfway begging. Offering themselves to him, because the call was irresistible despite being recognizable. They were moths who know what the light is, know what it will do to them. And come anyway.*

*Which is what made Whistling for them so addictive.*

*And so he gave them just a taste of what they craved. Let the Whistle just glide, first, a little ghost-caress down the pores of their skin.* There you go, little moths. One silky-soft brush of the end your whole being longs for, races toward, except the part that wakes.

*Leaving the club proved difficult. They kept screaming for more, not just the audience but the band, too, and one particularly alluring boy down front laid a paper orchid he'd fashioned out of a napkin on the lip of the stage. Such a brave, bold thing to do, for a boy in these parts. Any other Feeding time, and the Whistler would have knelt immediately, clutched such a present to his chest, led the supplicant to a quiet corner, and given what was asked. It was what he lived for, after all. To Whistle. To set them free. To promise, and then deliver.*

*But if he Fed, he knew, he'd be slower. Just that little bit less desperate. And that wouldn't do. Not with Mother. Especially since Mother already knew he was coming. Had to. Was too cagy and savage a predator not to.*

*And yet, Mother believed she still had time. Because the Whistler had believed she did, too, until just a few moments ago. And that was all the advantage he needed, as long as he played smart. And stayed hungry.*

*With a glance over his shoulder, one last locking of eyes with the orchid boy—so the boy would know just how sorry the Whistler was to be leaving, and so his heart would break—the Whistler slipped out the back of the club, across the parking lot, and away into the fetid Mississippi night.*

*It took some time to walk back to the motel, and he'd even lingered longer in the club than he realized. Because of the orchid boy, and because he was hungry. And because the thought of what he was about to do whipsawed through him like not even music had in such a long, long time. Was this grief, he wondered? Fear of change?*

*Or was it love? For his Destiny? My god, was this love?* Well, wait right where you are, Destiny, *he thought, and started to hum.* Wherever you are. I'll be back in the time it takes to break a heart. Nothing you can do to make me turn around.

*Across the empty highway from his hotel, in a shadowy stand of longleaf pines, the Whistler paused, just for a moment. Glancing up, he was astonished to see the faintest flush of pink at the very edge of the horizon, far out across the flats that fanned north from this place toward the delta. How long, he wondered, since he'd come this close to daylight? Since he'd so much as dreamed the world through which the waking walked? Cautiously, he stretched out his arm,* let the dawn coil, sleepily, around his skin. Immediately, the light penetrated, like poison sumac, and he felt the itch roar all the way up into his shoulder.

Goodnight, Mother, he thought to himself. Said to himself. And smiled, though he also did feel some sadness. At least, it seemed to him like sadness might have felt. Hello, Darkness. Old Friend. And hello, Destiny, out there somewhere, darting around in the last of the night like a newborn firefly, desperate and wild. Shooting off sparks. The way Mother told him he had, once.

Ducking his head, he scuttled across the roadway into the motel lot. Up the back stairs to the room Mother had rented them. Where she'd already be sleeping. Her last sleep.

He didn't wait. Didn't think. He threw open the door and leapt.

He knew, even before he landed, even as his teeth tore a throat-sized gash in the pillow and his fingers ripped the heart out of the mattress, that he was too late. And for one astonishing, mesmerizing second, for the first time in so very, very long, he felt himself freeze, his neck stretch helplessly into the dark, exposing itself even as his spine attempted to accordion his whole body shut while his brain fired conflicting impulses to his locked limbs to jump, run, duck, flee, scream. He was wildebeest again. Lion no longer. Vulnerable. Prey.

It felt fantastic.

Then the rest of the signals reached his brain. The empty air. The motionless shadows.

She wasn't here. She was gone. Mother was gone. He saw the note moments later, laid square on the table, held in place by the Gideon Bible. A last little joke.

Better hope you find her first, *the note read.* Although even that won't help you. Or her.

*With a growl that was at least half smile, the Whistler leapt back toward the open door, but stopped on the threshold. It had been too long since he'd touched the sun. It wouldn't kill him, he knew. But it would* hurt. *And he was out of practice with hurting.*

*Of course, so was Mother. So her head-start wouldn't amount to much. With half a dozen songs rising to his lips and his ears wide open to the world, he eased the door closed, sank down under the drawn curtains and crouched against the radiator. Someday soon, he thought. Whistled. To his Destiny, to Mother, he wasn't even sure which excited him more at that moment. It didn't matter, because he'd see them both. Be with them both. Someday.*

*Soon.*

### Got the Hungrys
### for Your Love

"Take the goddamn gun out of your mouth and give me a Juicy Fruit," Natalie snapped, jerking the wheel and sending the GTO skidding through yet another blind curve.

Sophie leaned back in her seat with the barrel of the gun on her tongue and the sea wind whipping through her hair. Another endless stretch of straight, three A.M.-road unspooled in front of them, and the car's headlights skimmed over its surface and into the surrounding pines like skipped stones. This evening, on the last ferry back from Cumberland, Natalie had felt the dry scratch of thirst in her throat catch and spread, until the entire cavern of her mouth seemed ablaze. Only the emptiness in her chest could distract her from the sensation. And only one person on Earth could have filled that.

And that one was safe with his grandmother, now. Somewhere gone.

"I thought you couldn't taste Juicy Fruit," Sophie mumbled around the gun. "Thought you didn't like that taste."

"Take the goddamn gun out of your mouth," Natalie snapped, and caught a glimpse of her own face in the rearview mirror. No paler or harder than usual. No more or less pretty, as far as she could tell. Just her face, with slack skin, empty eyes. And black, black, windblown hair. *Had her hair always been* that *black*?

Out of the corner of her eye, Natalie saw Sophie give the nozzle of the gun an obscene little tongue-flick before dropping it to her lap.

"Better?" she asked. "Madame Alligator-Bellow?"

"Juicy Fruit," said Natalie, clenching her teeth to keep from roaring.

Patting her hand around the glove box, Sophie found one last stick of gum curled into its foil wrapper like a dead caterpillar. She held it toward Natalie. "Ugh. Even touching it gives me the wallies, now."

"This from the woman last seen sucking a gun barrel." Natalie glanced down to unwrap the gum, and the car swerved onto the gravel shoulder before she caught the wheel with her knees.

"Watch your driving," Sophie said.

"So I can see the nothing when we hit it, you mean? Where the hell are we?"

"Natalie, seriously. Given that we're apparently going to be around for a long, long while, I'd like to have the use of my limbs. So I can run to my Roo, when you finally cave in and take us home."

Wrenching the wheel to the right, Natalie turned the car onto a dirt trail she'd barely registered as being there, and they bumped down it half a mile or more until the pines fell away. In front of them, three sand dunes humped out of the ground like whales surfacing. Natalie braked to a stop and shut off the car. For a while, they sat. In Natalie's throat, thirst crawled like a living thing. She half-believed she could hear her gums drying, cracking, like drywall flaking away. She held the wheel. Tried to think of a song, and not of Eddie.

"You know," Sophie said, "this gun? It's like a Lick Em Stick someone stuck a trigger on."

Slowly, with a long, hard sigh, Natalie turned. "What?"

"The gun." Sophie lifted it, waved it, put it next to her mouth. "It's like a Lick—"

"And there you have it. Congratulations, Sophie. The single most inane thing you have ever said. And I've been driving with you all night, every night, for almost a month."

"And sharing Moon Pies and tent-sleepovers for maybe twenty years before that." Sophie was smiling, sort of. A dried-out Sophie smile. Natalie closed her eyes, nodded, opened her eyes. "Not to mention *Gilmore Girls* reruns."

"Yep. And at least two boyfriends. Not counting the Whistler."

"I'm trying to block that one out."

"By all means. But yet you cannot deny. A gun is like a Lick Em Stick—"

"It isn't, though," Natalie exploded. Gratefully. Almost happily. Just

**90**

for the distraction. "It's nothing like a Lick Em Stick anyone stuck anything on. It couldn't be less like a Lick Em Stick if it were a…it's not even a stick. It's not even straight. And even if it were. Saying something's like something else just because it has sort of the same shape—or, in this case, not at all the same shape—is stupid. It's like saying a brain is like a sponge-blob someone stuck a thought in."

"Now, see, that's just cynical, that's what that is. It's worse. It's nihilistic."

"*Nihil*. Rhymes with bile."

"Oh. I thought it was *nil*. Rhymes with kill."

Natalie's slap rocked Sophie's head off her headrest into the door. Her other hand flew to her own mouth, and sound whistled from her lips. Wind through dead leaves.

"I'm sorry. Shit, Sophie. Sorry."

"Didn't hurt," Sophie mumbled, and sat up.

Natalie put a cold hand to her friend's cold cheek. "I really am sorry."

Sophie shrugged. "Nothing I haven't wanted to do to you."

"Really?"

"Are you kidding? Three weeks in a car, and you haven't let me play 'Sugar, Sugar' even one time?"

"Because it's a horrible song."

"It's the greatest song. It's what singing is for. You're my candy. I'm wanting you."

Even as she said that, Sophie seemed to register the words, and she barely whispered the last of them. Natalie thought about slapping her again. And also throwing her arms around her and holding on until the ocean came up the beach, over the dunes, and carried them off.

She did neither. Unconsciously, she fished in the pocket of her denim skirt and drew a cigarette from the crumpled pack. The second the cigarette touched her lips, she gagged and spit it out the window into the sand. "Well, hell," she said. "I apparently quit smoking, anyway."

"So there's one good thing already, see?" said Sophie, cheering immediately again. By force of will, Natalie realized, not nature. It had always been will. Knowing that made Natalie love her all the more.

"We should open a business," Natalie mumbled. "Just one visit from Nat and Soph. We'll cure your nasty habit once and for all. No matter what it is. Guaranteed to work."

"Hey! Natalie made a funny."

"Shut up."

Reedy sand-grass scratched against the side of the car. Over the dunes, stars dangled like mobiles.

"Nat," Sophie said, her voice falling again into a whisper, "let's just go find them. Just to *see*. We don't have to go inside or anything, I promise. I swear."

"Sophie, *I* swear, if you don't stop—"

"Just once. Just this one time. To say goodbye. God, Natalie, their faces. Their little feet."

Twisting the key hard, Natalie gunned the ignition, ground the car into reverse, turned them around, and set them bumping back up the trail. When they reached the asphalt, she fishtailed them onto it, their wheels kicking up a spray of dirt like a Jet Ski throwing wake. Then she floored the gas, and they roared off down the road between the pines.

"You hit some nothing," Sophie said. Then she lifted the gun off the seat and stuck the barrel back between her teeth.

Sometime well after midnight, Natalie pulled the car into the parking lot of a Waffle House on the outskirts of a town with no other visible lights. Sophie glanced up in surprise. The building was low and brick. Teenagers crowded around two booths near the front, and a couple of solitary trucker-types sipped coffee at the counter. Through the grime and the flittering moths on the windows, all of them looked yellow.

Sophie fabricated a yawn. "Where are we?"

Yawning, Natalie thought. There was something she wouldn't have expected to miss. "We're at Waffle House," she said.

With a roll of her eyes, Sophie somehow mustered yet another grin. "Thanks, Sparky. Waffle House where?"

"Waffle House is its own where. No matter where it is."

"That's good. I like that. That should be like their slogan. *We're our own where.*"

"This just seemed…as good a place as any." And with her hands trembling on the wheel, she turned to Sophie and caught her eye. "Right?"

It took a moment for Sophie to understand. But only a moment. One of her legs began to bob up and down. Her hands, Natalie noticed, were trembling, too. "Oh, shit, Nat." Her tongue snuck out onto her lips. "Here? Tonight? You think? I mean…it's really time?"

Natalie lifted her hands off the wheel. The shaking, she realized, was at least as much hunger as panic. Or, no. It was more. Almost all hunger. The realization made her want to weep. But it didn't make her less hungry. She put her hands in her hair.

"I don't know, Sophie. How do we know? It just…feels like it's time."

"I'm calling your mom," Sophie said, and before Natalie could even process that, or do anything but blink in surprise, Sophie grabbed the stolen cell phone from the glove box and left the car, walking fast across the empty highway into the shadows of the pines.

Scrambling out of her seat, Natalie stood to give chase, a growl rising in her throat and momentarily overwhelming even the hunger. But then she just clutched her open door and held on, staring at Sophie's back. She watched Sophie's fingers pushing buttons. The phone rising to her ear. Her mother's phone had to be ringing by now. Wherever her mother was. Or else her voice was already in Sophie's ear.

Or else her son's voice was.

*Don't answer,* she thought, while tears crept up behind her eyes again. Even they felt cold, now.

And then, *Answer, Mom. Please.*

Sophie turned around. Her hand with the phone dropped to her hip. "Not her number anymore," she said. "That bitch changed her number. And took my Roo."

Half-lurching, half-skipping, Natalie moved fast across the road. A grin she didn't have to muster spread across her lips. *Thank you, Mom,* she was thinking. *Wherever you are. Wherever you've taken my son.* She grabbed the phone out of Sophie's hand, held it up, and they both stared at it for a few seconds, as though it were a heart she'd ripped out. Her own, Sophie's. What difference did it make? She slammed the phone to the pavement and stomped it to pieces.

When she looked up a few seconds later, she found Sophie looking not at her but over her shoulder. Slowly, Natalie turned and saw the trucker.

Just a boy, really. A long, lanky Southern boy, with skin like a slick summer peach and an alligator smile he hadn't mastered and didn't yet mean. "Well, damn," he said, and then the full force of what he was looking at hit him, and his smile went slack.

Natalie felt a twinge. A real and painful one. What a good and aching night this was turning out to be. And now it would get so much better. And worse. *Stop right there,* she wanted to tell him. This boy, who didn't yet realize where he'd wandered. *Turn around. Run.*

But she knew she'd tell him no such thing. Not tonight.

"*Thelma and Louise*," Sophie whispered by her side, and Natalie jerked.

"What?"

"*Thelma and Louise*. Taking back the night. Look at him. He's perfect. He *wants* us to come over there. And there's no one else here to see."

"Sophie…"

"Look at that little hunting look he's giving us. Who'd miss him?"

*I would*, Natalie thought, knowing that made no sense and probably wasn't even true, and stepped forward, letting the full glow of the streetlight bathe her. Letting the boy see. Even ten feet away, she could feel him vibrate like a string she'd struck.

"Well, damn," the boy said again, swaying.

"Don't," Natalie murmured, and took another step. Then another. He was still five feet away, but she could taste his breath on the night air, bubble-gummed and maple-syrupped and hot with him. She could feel—*taste*—the condensation on his arms, in the hollow of his throat, against her lips. Could feel the life surging through him. It was as though she'd developed a new shark-sensitivity to every twitching, desperate, useless sensation living things emitted.

"Don't," she said again, and moved closer still.

"But I want to," he said. So close, now. His mouth so near. Cheeks no longer yellow, but sweetly tan and red against the dark.

"So do I," Natalie said.

Sophie edged up beside her, hip knocking against Natalie's like a train car coupling. *"Thelma and Louise. Thelma and Louise."*

With a snarl that almost staggered trucker-boy, almost drove him to his knees, Natalie grabbed Sophie by the wrist and yanked her past him, past the GTO, and across the parking lot. She had to pull hard, because Sophie was trying to dig her feet into the pavement, and from her mouth came a *mewing* Natalie had never heard before. She allowed herself a single glance back, saw the kid staring after them, leaning toward them, his desire unfurling like a sail. She practically had to hurl Sophie into the restaurant while holding the door with her hip.

For a second, she thought Sophie was going to turn on her, that they were going to have it out right here, once and for all. But then—like a whisper from an angel, a breath from God—Waffle House washed over them. So stupidly soothing. Familiar in a way almost nothing else had been, from the moment she'd awoken in the back seat of Sophie's car the morning after they'd met the Whistler. The fluorescents not so much glowing as blaring. The jukebox blasting Buck Owens. The dead-eyed, anemic counterwoman halfway smiling and nodding them toward a booth without ever really seeing them. All they had to do was...act naturally.

Sophie whimpered. Just a regular whimper, not mewing. She tapped Natalie's shoulder, pointed at the counter. A few stools down from the nearest trucker sat a woman, her head wrapped in brightly colored green and turquoise scarves. Next to her sat her daughter, aged ten at most, busily feeding her French fries. Stuffing them in little fistfuls into her mother's mouth and laughing. Maps lay spread on the counter in front of them, held in place by ketchup bottles. The woman tucked a stray strand of hair behind her daughter's ear, sighed, laughed back. Natalie's mouth formed an O.

"Well, okay. Hi, y'all," Sophie said to the teens in the front booth, and Natalie jerked her attention away from the counter.

The teens were staring, of course. The girls, too, though the wan little redhead in the back seemed to be trying to force her eyes down to the table while she played, pitifully, with her napkin. She looked like a French fry dipped in ketchup, barely noticeable even right in front of you. And she knew it. God, Natalie remembered that sensation. Whole Saturdays traipsing around the Goodwills of Charlotte with her mother, trying to find clothes to bring out the blue in her eyes, the only part of her Natalie actually thought *might* be attractive. Once, not more than a year ago, sitting half-drunk on lawn chairs in front of their trailer while Eddie gurgled on her lap, Jess had announced, out of nowhere, "It's so sad. Pathetic. The way none of us realizes what really makes us pretty, or sexy, until it's way too late to be any use. Any use that's good for us, anyway. One more proof of just how much God hates women."

It was the acid in her mother's voice, more than the pronouncement, that had made Natalie look up from her baby. Half-moon bright overhead. Trees bending in the fresh spring wind. A rare, work-free evening unfolding in front of her. Baseball on the radio. "How's that?" she'd said.

Her mother had just settled deeper into her slump in her chair, eyes too big behind her glasses. A bullfrog on a lily pad.

"God. Hates. Women."

Natalie had lifted her son to her shoulder, burped him, squeezed him tight. "This here," she'd said. Stroking her son. "This proves otherwise."

And Jess just sat a while. Eventually, she'd reached out, not for the baby, but for her own daughter's cheek. Then she'd shaken her head. "That proves He loves *Eddie*."

*Poor little French fry girl*, Natalie thought now. *I could make them look at you differently. Just by making* you *look at you differently.*

Grabbing Sophie's wrist again, she tugged her to the counter. And on impulse, because the anemic waitress just happened to be standing there, Natalie ordered a double patty melt to go.

"Hey," Sophie said. "That sounds so good." She ordered one, too. Behind them, Natalie could hear the teenagers shifting on the vinyl seats, starting to fall back into themselves.

Patsy succeeded Buck on the jukebox, "Walkin' After Midnight." Sophie grabbed the nearest salt and pepper shakers and started making clip-clops to the beat. "You know," she said, "a patty melt's like a dead thing someone slapped cheese and onions on."

Natalie's gaze had returned to the woman and her daughter, just a few stools down. Banter with Sophie came so easily. Like so many things, if you let them. All she had to do was let them. Right? "That doesn't work at all," she said.

"Why not?"

"It's not a metaphor. It's not even a comparison. It's just what it is."

"Well, there's the difference between you and me, Nat. You worry about what things mean. I just say what they are."

"I think I'll go throw up, now," Natalie murmured, and was startled when Sophie leaned in by her ear.

"Have to eat something, first." Then the woman in the scarf turned and touched her hand.

Natalie was so surprised that she almost swatted the woman off her stool. She also thought she might melt, Wicked Witch of the West-style. Nothing left but a pool of ketchup.

"Oh, honey," the woman said. "You're just like me."

That stunned even Sophie to silence. Together, they stared at the woman's head, the strands of stringy auburn and gray hair sneaking out from under the scarves.

"What do you mean?" Natalie whispered.

"Cold all the time," the woman said, and rubbed Natalie's hand between her own. "You're so cold. I could tell just by looking at you. I can't ever get warm. Want your fortune read?"

Natalie glanced toward Sophie, back to the woman. "Huh?"

"I like her," Sophie murmured. "She speaks my language."

From the other side of the woman, the daughter leaned forward, chin in her palm, sighing and smiling. "Just let her do it. No one's let her do it for days. No *paying* customers for a week. She needs the practice. I'm going to the bathroom, Mom." Hopping off the stool, the girl wandered toward the back of the restaurant.

The counterwoman returned with their burgers in a bag. Natalie took the bag, turned to go, but Sophie grabbed her shoulders and pushed her down onto the stool.

"Give her good news," Sophie said to the woman. "She could use some."

Beaming, the woman produced a deck of cards from somewhere in her skirt and shuffled them. "Well, then, let's find her some. It's always there, somewhere."

For a fortune teller, the woman proved a lousy card-shuffler. And she'd just fanned the deck on top of the maps on the counter when her cell phone went off. Wincing, the woman reached into another pocket, pulled out an iPhone, stared at the screen.

"Oy," she said, and silenced the phone.

"Not good news?" Natalie found herself asking.

The woman had avoided looking right at them, Natalie realized. Even once. As if she knew better. *Or could help herself? Could any of them really do that?*

With a shrug, the woman pushed some of her hair back into her scarf, smoothed the exhaustion lines in her forehead. "Depends when you ask me, I suppose. Isn't that always the way with men?"

*Not in my case,* Natalie thought.

The woman gestured at the cards. "Touch two. Don't turn them over."

Natalie did, and the woman set those cards aside, then reshuffled and fanned the cards open again. "And two more."

Natalie touched two more.

The woman smiled, glanced over her shoulder toward the bathroom in search of her daughter. For a horrified second, Natalie realized she'd lost track of Sophie, half-stood, then spotted her friend a few stools down, hunched over, peering into one of the mini-jukeboxes.

"Good," said the woman. "Okay. Let's see what we can know." She turned over a card. A black ace. She flipped a second black ace. Started to turn the third, then left it face down. Her fingers drummed the top of it, and her smile twitched.

Natalie felt her whole body tense. Her voice came out as a bobcat's murmur. "That's not funny. You have no idea how not funny—"

"Sorry," said the woman, rolling her eyes at herself, smiling. "Did it wrong. Forgot to cut. Jesus, I'm out of practice. As my smart-mouth daughter told you. Let me just reshuffle, and we'll…"

As she pulled the cards to her, though, Natalie saw her check the fourth one. So casually. Her smile vanished completely.

The moment it did, giggling exploded behind her. Natalie looked up just in time to see the woman's daughter hurtle past, yelling, "Sorry, Mom, sorry Scary Cold Lady, couldn't resist." Then she was out the door of the Waffle House into the night.

After a stunned few seconds, the woman in the scarves stood and started to fold the maps in front of her. Natalie glanced at Sophie, then back to the woman. The woman shook her head. Sighed. Flipped the deck so Natalie could see. Every single card was a black ace.

"I'm sorry," the woman said. "She thinks she's hilarious. Thinks she's Tina Fucking Fey. I hope I didn't scare you."

Out the window, Natalie could see the girl turning cartwheels in the parking lot. When she saw her mother looking, she waved.

"She...*is* pretty hilarious," Natalie said. Thinking of her son's gurgle. Seeing his smile.

"You're not kidding," said Sophie, in the same, rueful tone, and Natalie knew she was thinking the same thoughts. The woman—and her daughter—really had shown them their futures, after all. The ones they weren't going to have, no matter how much future they got.

The woman took a ten-dollar bill from her purse and laid it next to Natalie. "For your patty melts," she said. "And your patience." She left.

Absently, automatically, Sophie and Natalie both unwrapped their burgers and slathered them in ketchup. By the time they got outside, the woman and daughter were gone. The trucker-boy, too. Luckily for all of them. In the car, Natalie switched on the radio and started punching through the stations until she found Loretta, sending 'em all to Fist City.

"Now, this," she said through her hunger, through the image of the scarf-woman's daughter cartwheeling through the dark. "'Fist City', Not 'Sugar Sugar.' *This* is what singing is for."

Sophie clucked her tongue. "Anger. You need to find a healthy outlet for that."

"Shut up," said Natalie, and pulled them out of the lot.

George Jones on the radio now, singing flat and sad, no drama at all. Like he wasn't even a person at all, just a disembodied feeling. About a girl he used to know.

"The daughter can't be Tina Fey," Sophie muttered.

"Tina what?"

"That woman. She said her daughter thinks she's Tina Fey. But if she were Tina Fey, something would have gone wrong when she substituted the cards. Complications would have ensued."

"Complications?"

"Hello? Ground control to Major Natalie Robot. Switch brain back to On position. Over."

"We have to get rid of these burgers," Natalie said.

Sophie let out an explosive sigh. "My God, yes, even the smell is giving me the wallies."

"The *willies*, goddamnit. Willies."

"I know."

"Then why not say it? What's wrong with the willies?"

"I like my Willie," Sophie said quietly. "I miss him so."

Natalie twitched so hard that she almost rocketed them off the road. Because she'd actually forgotten. Sophie hadn't called her son by his real name in so long that Natalie had stopped knowing what it was.

She glanced toward her friend. Sophie was crying. "You've got to stop doing that, Hon." She touched Sophie's cheek. "You've got to stop thinking about it. They're gone."

"I won't let it happen, Nat. I won't let it. I can't."

"It's happened. It's done."

"Natalie," Sophie said, and instead of a whimper, that new, mewing sound spilled from her lips. "I'm so hungry."

"I know."

"We have to choose."

"I know."

"Anyone you want, Nat. Any*where* you want. We can be super-heroes. Eat only bad guys. Or we can just pick a time, and wherever we are, whoever we meet at that precise moment, or whatever. I trust you. We can—"

"Seriously, Sophie," Natalie barked. "I'm serious, now. You want to lay this on me? You want me to have to live with the choice? What do *you* suggest? Come on, I want to hear it. Next breakdown victim we come across, maybe? Next dude in bad pants? Oh, I know, how about next black dude, you always told me you were going to try a black dude someday."

"That's just mean," Sophie sniffled.

"You're goddamn right."

"Natalie, it's killing me. And you."

"Maybe we should let it."

"He said that wouldn't work. He said instinct would take over. Remember?"

"He said a lot of things. Maybe we're stronger than he is."

"Maybe you are, Nat."

And suddenly, for the first time since it had happened, Natalie remembered his face. Could *see* it hovering over her. That mouth, so red and round. Already dripping with her. The pull of him overwhelming, sucking in every bit of her like a black hole. And yet all she'd wanted, at that moment—*my God, she wanted it still*—was for him to keep kissing her. Devouring her.

No. She'd wanted to feed herself to him.

*What will it be like?* she'd asked while he fed. Not actually caring.

And he'd surprised her by pausing momentarily, as though between courses. As though he'd never considered the question before. Or— wait—as though he'd thought of little else.

*Like...*he'd whispered. Staring at her. At motionless Sophie, on whose thighs Natalie lay. *Like...coming home. Like letting go. Of all those little, stupid feelings and sensations you think matter so much. Until you just slip away. Same thing that happens to everyone before they die. Only you'll still be you. And you won't die.*

He'd been right about all of it, too. Except the letting go. How was she supposed to do that? And what did one hold on to, afterward? Was it really possible to be alive and just ride the night wind, forever, like bacteria or a spore? Was it possible to stay living and stop thinking?

Was thinking what killed people, in the end?

"Natalie," Sophie whimpered.

"Ssh." She leaned back, closed her eyes, felt the car hurtling them into the blankness. Felt it carrying them where it would. Bacteria. Spore.

"Natalie, please. Let's go home."

Natalie opened her eyes just in time to see the deer's flank as they slammed into it. The animal's head snapped sideways and the antlers banged down on the hood so hard that the GTO's back wheels came off the asphalt momentarily. Natalie jammed on the brake, but the deer stayed stuck, bumping and banging up and down as the car shuddered and screamed, and then it slid down the grille, bones booming as they splintered beneath the tires like 4th of July firecrackers. Even as the car skidded to a sideways stop, Natalie knew there was still a part of the animal trapped in the rear tires, its weight like a trailer pull, dragging them.

"Oh my God," Sophie whined. "Oh my God."

Natalie squeezed the steering wheel until her knuckles threatened to explode through her skin. With a grunt, she made herself let go, drew her hands into her lap.

"You hit it," Sophie said.

"You think?"

"Is it dead?"

Natalie opened her mouth to give that the answer it deserved, then froze. She turned to Sophie, stared into her eyes. Sophie shrank back.

It took her an absurdly, almost endearingly long time before she understood.

Natalie wasn't sure, but she thought the mewing was coming from her own throat now as she and Sophie both spun to their doors, wrenched them open, and leapt from the car. The animal was a splayed, shredded ruin locked to the bumper, its head bent up under the rear axle and its antlers shattered all over the road. Natalie and Sophie dove together into the pumping gore in its crumpled ribs like little kids swooping for candy in a burst piñata. Blood saturated Natalie's skirt, pooled around her thighs, so warm. She knelt atop a rib and snapped it as she plunged her face down, almost banging her forehead against Sophie's. The sound Sophie was making might have been laughter. As she buried her face in the spurting liquid, spitting aside hairy skin, Natalie reached out and stroked her friend's hair.

Sophie straightened first. Natalie followed moments later, settling back on her haunches, fingers still twisted in Sophie's hair. Gently, she disentangled them and let go. Sophie's face twisted up, and she kept spitting, over and over, trying to clear the taste from her lips and teeth. Natalie just wiped a disgusted hand repeatedly across her own mouth. Still kneeling in the mangled deer, they stared at each other.

"So…" Sophie finally said, glancing down once more at the animal and then back at Natalie. "We're vegetarians?"

Natalie closed her eyes, shuddered, opened her eyes.

"Humanitarians?" Sophie said.

They stood together, arms around each other, bits of cartilage clinging to their skin, their legs and skirts dripping. Natalie was about to return to the car when Sophie's hands tightened on her arms.

"Nat. You need to hear me. I'm going home now."

"Sophie. We talked about this."

"You talked about it. Stop glaring. Stop pretending you're better and wiser and just be my friend and listen. For both our sakes."

"Okay," Natalie whispered, going completely still. Merle on the car radio, spilling gently out on the open driver's side door. Singing, "Mama Tried."

"Just listen. I know why you think we need to run. I know you think you're saving our Roos. But I've been thinking. A lot. It's almost all I've thought about since we left. Except eating. And mostly, I haven't even been thinking about that. Natalie. Seriously. What better gift could a mother give her children?"

Natalie felt her jaw drop. Held her ground. Held to the Earth.

"Think about it. Seriously. I'm serious. I can't stop. He's all I ever think about. His little feet. God, his little feet. We could be back there in, what, five hours? And never leave them again. Ever."

"You have to stop, Sophie. Please. You have to—"

"What did you want for Eddie when Eddie was born, Natalie? What did you think you could do for him? What did you want to give him? How about no worries, ever? How about no pain? *Ever.*"

"Sophie. I can't hear this. I—"

"How about no dying? You can go or not go, Natalie. But I'm going. With or without—"

It was like a cobra strike, Natalie thought seconds later, her teeth still buried in the softness under her best friend's chin, Sophie's body twitching helplessly underneath her. Like a goddamn bolt of lightning, Natalie thought as she drank. The only concern she'd had at the instant she'd acted was that it would taste like the deer, make her wretch. That she wouldn't be able to finish.

And it tasted cold, all right. Sour. Not quite right. But it was bearable. Fine. She lapped away, more slowly now, burying her face deeper in Sophie's throat, rocking side to side to Merle's rhythm.

It tasted fine.

PART TWO

## I Fall

## to Pieces

Or rather, she realized a good minute or so later, still straddling Sophie's body and gulping greedily at her blood, it didn't make her retch. The fizzless blood wasn't pumping, of course, so she had to suck it to her lips, using the shredded jugular like a straw, and the taste had the ghost of actual flavor in it, but old and fizzles, like a flat Coke. Also, it did about as much to slake her thirst as swallowing her own saliva. She straightened again.

Under her, against her thighs, Sophie's body still twitched faintly. But not with life. More like a pile of leaves she'd stirred, slowly going still. A sob rose in her throat. Natalie let it come, made herself bend her head and stare down into her best friend's face. Still wide-eyed, too round, glowing. Gone. Sitting back on her haunches, Natalie looked away from Sophie, down the road between the pines, up into the blank, black sky.

A wave of panic lifted her to her feet, set her staggering away only to slip in a paddy of deer-innards and fall hard on her back, smacking her head against the tarmac. She lay there, dazed, wetness welling through her skirt and blouse, willing a truck to come and crush her. She also wanted her hand to move itself out of the gristly, stringy goo it had clutched as she fell, but was unable to do anything but lie there, open-mouthed, sucking in the truth as though it could sustain her.

She had been a mother, and wasn't one, now. A daughter, too. She'd had a lifelong best friend. And eaten her.

And she was still hungry.

*Was this all there was, now? What else could there be? Apparently, she could lure living people to her without trying, without consequences. And precisely because of that, she could never draw any sustenance from them except by devouring them, ripping their precious, fragile, anguished, wasted lives from them.*

*Or listening to them sing.*

With a snarl that was half-shriek, Natalie shoved herself to a sitting position, brought a hand to her face to wipe her lips and instead smeared cold deer-insides over them, shrieked again, and stumbled to her feet and toward the car. She had only two thoughts left. The only two thoughts she would ever have, for as long as she had any: music, and motion. Music and motion.

And eating. But she wouldn't think about eating.

Wrenching her door open, she fell into the driver's seat, not looking back, not looking back, she didn't have to, she would see Sophie's guile-less eyes widening—*in welcome?*—at the instant Natalie lunged for her for the rest of her life. Forever. She tried to twist the key in the GTO's ignition, but instead knocked it out of the slot onto the floor mat.

By the time her fingers found it, she was gabbling nonsense words, fragments of half-song she'd sung to herself while walking to work, coos she'd burbled to Eddie while leaning over his bassinet. Shivers wracked her body, wracked while her dry tongue and throat dried further and the emptiness outside sucked at her like a vacuum. She jammed the key in place, twisted the car to life, and without even straightening, floored the gas, so that the thump from right beside her almost launched her through the windshield. Slamming on the brakes and wrestling the wheel, Natalie banged her ribs into the door as the GTO lurched, skidded sideways, straightened, almost tilted all the way over on its side, and went still. Rumbling.

*What had she hit? Deer, probably, its legs or something, part of it still stuck to the grille.*

Except the thump had been at her window. Practically right up against her cheek. She turned her head and saw the side-view mirror dangling, reflector-side down, like an ear halfway ripped off.

*Drive,* she thought, even as her hands came off the wheel and her head, seemingly all on its own, swung the rest of the way around.

Sophie stood in the center of the road. One hand raised, as though waving goodbye. As Natalie stared, the waving hand tipped all the way back on its wrist, flopped sickeningly behind, until Sophie used her other hand to straighten it. Tree shadows seemed to crisscross around her, not quite touching her, and they did nothing to hide the ruin of her throat where Natalie had torn it out. Her head wasn't sitting quite right, either. Not sideways, exactly. Just no longer connected properly. Like a cut flower propped back on its stem. She just stood there, waving, bloody dress cleaving to her and the moonlight bathing her.

Natalie was out of the car, almost skipping, and had covered half the distance back to Sophie before instinct stopped her. Survival sense.

*Should she be scared?*

Sophie still stood there. Hand raised. Natalie's teeth-marks like a necklace around her throat, strung with little blood-pearls.

To her surprise, Natalie realized that she'd raised her own arms, now. To defend herself, if need be. As she watched, Sophie's head tilted a little to the right. *Because Sophie was cocking it? Or was it coming loose?*

Or was that a challenge?

*Let it be*, Natalie snarled inside her own head. If it came, she wouldn't fight any more than Sophie had. Even so, forcing her arms back down to her sides felt like prying apart steel doors. She tilted her own head sideways, just enough to catch Sophie's eyes and hold them. Then she started forward. With each step, her body tensed for an onslaught. Somewhere deep in her brain, something was screaming, but whether that was vampire-Natalie fearing for its life or whatever was left of the woman she'd been still keening over its death, she couldn't tell. She didn't much care. Her mouth kept forming her best friend's name, but she couldn't seem to get it all the way out. It came as a jumble, equal parts "Soph" and "so" and "sorry" and a sob.

She kept walking. And Sophie kept watching. Bright eyes still bright, maybe just with starlight. Hand lifted, as though Natalie were still leaving.

Slowly, slowly, Natalie reached out and touched Sophie's arm. Sophie didn't so much as blink, or even lower her waving hand. Natalie lowered it for her. It came down a little too easily, like a stripped gear.

"Soph," Natalie managed, and pushed at her friend's blood-matted hair. "You're still here." Throwing her arms around Sophie's shoulders, Natalie pulled her friend against her. Even as she did, she felt her neck tense for the bite, her whole body tremble as Sophie's face, then teeth, settled against her throat.

And didn't tear. Didn't rip. Just rested there.

"I'm so sorry," Natalie murmured, weeping, holding tight. "I had to. I had to. I'm sorry." Against her hip, Natalie felt one of Sophie's hands jerk, then settle on her back. Even then, the embrace felt more like holding a Sophie-doll than Sophie. Natalie held on anyway.

Finally, after a long time, and without letting go, she turned and started to draw them both toward the GTO. "Come on," she said. Half-sang. As though talking to her son. "Let's clean you up. Oh, God, I'm so sorry. Come on."

When she had her friend settled and leaned in to pull the shoulder hardness across Sophie's chest, she accidentally jostled her shoulder, and Sophie's head tipped sideways, started to stretch loose on its last tendons, and Natalie had to grab it and tilt it back, until it sat almost straight. She was afraid to take her hand away. If she did, she thought the head might roll clean off.

*And come to rest in her lap? Still blinking at her? Would she still be Sophie then? Assuming she still was now?*

Again, somehow, Natalie stopped thinking. She pulled her hand away, and Sophie's head stayed put, roughly where it belonged, staring down the empty road into the dark. Natalie slammed the door and returned to the driver's seat, checking the tires for deer-bits. She saw lots of spatter, but nothing protruding.

"Okay," she said, settling, keying the ignition. "Come on. Let's get clean. Find somewhere to rest." She put the car in Drive and drove.

For a while, she couldn't even make herself glance at the passenger seat. She was afraid that when she did, she'd discover that she was alone after all. That what had risen off the road was not monster-Sophie, not even ghost- or zombie-Sophie, but the dying remnants of her. The last Sophie there would ever be. The thought of losing her again was more than Natalie could bear.

But when she did look—in the rearview mirror, first, then directly— she saw Sophie still sitting up. One of her hands lay turned upward in her lap, the fingers twitching. She had a strand of what Natalie first thought was bloody hair and then realized was neck-tendon in her mouth, so that she could suck on it.

Given the grue she'd practically bathed in this night, the sight proved more pathetic than disgusting. Gently, she reached over and tugged the tendon free. "Honey, don't do that," she murmured, and stroked Sophie's cold, red-streaked cheek.

Overhead, the sky showed a first hint of pink, like an eye just coming open. There were woods to either side, probably dense enough to keep the harshest light off them. But wherever they were, it wasn't Cumberland Island. Someone would stumble across them. And today, in her current state, and with Sophie in her current condition—whatever it was—that would be fatal. Plain and simple. Quite possibly for everyone involved. They passed a billboard for some hotel. *Red Backer, Red Cracker*, Natalie didn't quite catch the name. But it had to be ahead, and not too far.

"See, Soph?" Her voice had an ugly buzz despite the various fluids she'd sucked down tonight. A frantic, fly-on-windscreen rasp. "It's all right. We're close." She reached out to pat Sophie's thigh and caught sight of the blood caked all the way up her own arm. Even she had no idea whether her laugh was hysterical. "Only, maybe…gas station first, huh? One with restrooms around back and one of those nice, rusty sinks and that stink you always loved so well? I mean *love*."

When Sophie didn't so much as turn, Natalie reached under her seat and came up with Sophie's pink and yellow canvas purse. Same one she'd had since high school, with little Sophie-slogans inked in pink and purple all over it. *RC Girl. Slurp Me Up, Scotty.* And down at the bottom along the pink stitching, *NatQueenCold. Forever.*

From eleventh grade, that one. From the night Natalie had lured the DJ at one of their lame-o high school dances into the hallway, then locked him out of the gym, hijacked his sound system, and played "Stardust" and "Autumn Leaves" until her baffled schoolmates booed her offstage.

Not even ten years ago. Hardly any time at all.

Trembling, she shoved her free hand into the bag, rooted around, came up with a Dixie Chicks tape, threw that in the back. On the second try, she found what she was looking for. Fumbling the cassette out of its case, Natalie started to push it into the dashboard deck, then stopped, staring at the J-card in her other hand.

"Jesus Christ, Sophie. How many versions of this do you have on here?"

All the way down both columns of the card, Sophie had written the same words, over and over. *Sugar, Sugar. Sugar, Sugar. Sugar, Sugar.*

"Is this all Archies? Or are there really that many different people who've sung this?" Amazingly, despite everything, despite the dried-blood coating on her lips that cracked as it happened, Natalie grinned. "Maybe it really *is* a great song." And as she pushed the tape into the deck, and her smile slipped, she wondered just how many times this would have to happen before she learned. All their lives, Natalie had believed — *known* — she had better taste than Sophie. In boys. Food. Life and work choices. Baby-clothes. Music, most of all. How many moments like this would it take before she understood, once and for all, that she was wrong?

The first sounds out of the speakers weren't the Archies. Natalie was so startled that a full minute of grinding guitar-piano crunch pounded by before she recognized it. "That's not 'Sugar, Sugar'," she said, starting to laugh again. "That's my Velvets. That's 'Waiting for My —'"

Voices exploded in a candy-colored fireworks dazzle. The Archies, all right. *Sugar, Sugar,* laid on top of "Waiting for My Man." A mash-up from hell. A stroke of serious genius. Sweetness and glee pasted over the grimiest, grungiest riff of the sixties. Natalie threw her head back, floored the accelerator, laughed outright, screamed that two-word hook as it repeated and repeated and repeated, swiveled in her seat to throw an arm around Sophie and pull her close.

Then her voice left her completely. The music, too, seemed to evaporate as it hit the air, the color gone out of it. Just noise and smoke.

Sophie had slumped in her seat. Eyes still open, staring straight ahead. Head tilting too far to the right. Only the twitch in her upturned fingers confirmed that any part of her was still there.

Natalie punched the tape out of the deck, slammed the radio off. "Right," she said. "Hang on, Soph. Please, please, please."

On and on the road ran, through trees and more trees. Past old sheds sinking into themselves like rotting gingerbread houses, farm fields with their ridged rows of dirt humping up twisted and blue in the pre-dawn gray like varicose veins. No Waffle House, no gas station. *How could there possibly be this much road through this much nowhere and no fucking gas stations, even in Georgia?*

Right as the light began to burn Natalie's eyes—or, really, eye*lids*—and she was seriously considering turning the GTO straight off the road, through the yellow wildflowers that had lined their way for the last 50 miles or so, and as deep into the woods as it would go, buildings appeared in front of them. Three, side by side. A McDonald's, a Red Whatever-the-Hell hotel, a nameless gas station with the light on inside its pitiful little market and not so much as a pick-up parked out front. The roadside flowers rolled right up to the paving. Their own private yellow brick road, leading them to Oz. Now all they needed to do was *not* see the Wizard, or anyone else. And never get home.

"Look," she said in her new rasp, taking Sophie's freezing, upturned hand in her slightly warmer one. "Bathrooms around back, even. We're safe, Soph. I'll get you safe."

She parked the GTO on the far right-hand edge of the lot, well out of the dim glow from the fluorescents that buzzed over the gas pumps. When she got out, she could see the guy working the counter inside the mini-mart, green corduroy cap worn backward on his head and stringy hair the color of road gravel. Whatever he had on the stereo, he was air-guitaring to it. She couldn't see his eyes because he was too deep in his solo to look up, or else he hadn't even heard them. So much the better.

Hurrying around the car, she opened the passenger side door, tried to wedge Sophie's head against her hip so it wouldn't come loose as Natalie eased her out of the car. But the second Natalie shifted her, whole sections of Sophie seemed to slip, jostle sideways, as though she were a Sophie-shaped potato sack.

"*Damn* it," Natalie whispered, using every inch of her body to hold her friend in the car seat. "Just…stay there. Shit." She got Sophie upright again, leaned against the top of the car, and put her forehead down on the metal, which was somehow already slick with dew.

Or, more likely, blood, Natalie realized. Hers. Sophie's. The deer's. Enough to paint the whole GTO red, if she ever felt Georgia enough to do that. In her shoulders, exhaustion settled, heavier than any she remembered feeling back when she'd actually needed sleep. It spread down her arms into her hips. For just a second, she panicked, thought maybe it was the sun affecting her, that she was turning to stone or something.

Then she straightened, glanced toward air-guitar guy, and shook her head hard. "Okay. Soph. Stay right there, okay? Don't move. I'm too tired to drag you." *Also, you're doing this pulling-apart thing that's making me a little nervous.* "I'm going to wash off so I can get us into that hotel over there. Then I'll see to you. Okay? Two minutes. Do you want the tape back on?"

How Sophie had managed to get the frayed neck-tendon back between her lips, Natalie had no idea. "You know," Natalie said, "that's really kind of…"

But in a way, she supposed it was a good sign. Not as good as breaking into full-throated Archies harmony, but a start. A sign of life. Or hunger, anyway. She drummed once on the car hood. "Right. You enjoy that. I'll just…two minutes. I love you, Sophie."

The bathroom proved surprisingly spotless. Only the ammonia smell made her gag as she bent over the sink, turned the water on as hot as it would go, and shoved her arms underneath it. It felt even better than Natalie had imagined it would. She began to rake at the crusted blood on her arms with her nails, peeling it back, scratching all the way down under the first layer of skin. It hurt, but gloriously, sweetly. Like living did. Had. On impulse, she ducked her whole head, somehow wedged it sideways under the tap and let the spurt of scalding water cascade through her hair, over her eyes, down her mouth, the heat like sunshine, almost. Like daylight. Like the memory of daylight.

She didn't fall asleep. Not really. But she did lose track, just for those wet, warm moments, of where she was. Sensation overwhelmed her, suffused and soothed her. When she remembered, she twisted off the tap with a long sigh, but without any panic, and stood up. There were no towels, just an air-dryer. That would take too long, she reasoned. Although it wasn't like Sophie was going anywhere.

Whistling without even recognizing the tune, shaking her whole, sopping self like a puppy, she stepped out of the bathroom, winced at the spreading sunrise overhead, and got within three steps of the car before she realized she'd been wrong about that.

The GTO's passenger door was open. And Sophie was gone.

*Had she ever even been there?* Natalie stared, mouth open, all that heat already evaporating through her skin like steam because her skin could no longer hold it. Shivering, she took a step forward, made herself blink, tried to clear her head, and realized she could hear music.

"Sugar, Sugar," the original version, blaring out of the car stereo. So Sophie really had been here. And couldn't have gone far. Couldn't have. Couldn't have. Natalie stumbled forward another few steps, looked frantically down the road in both directions, then across the street toward the trees. *The light,* she thought. *She'd gotten herself out of the light. It probably hurt even more on open wounds.* Then she glanced over her shoulder into the mini-mart.

Sophie stood just inside the glass doors, legs apart, eyes straight ahead toward the cans of chewing tobacco on the wall behind the counter. Head tilting over. Bits of tendon and vein creeping out of her neck like weeds through cracked sidewalk. Blood-caked skirt hiked to her hips, so that the counter-guy could get his head all the way up under. He was still wearing his corduroy cap.

"Oh, God, Sophie," Natalie moaned. She supposed she should be happy. But the protective shadows around her were lifting away, and the light hurt all over. And she was so very, very tired. Lost and tired. And sad. "Come on, Soph," she called, not even sure Sophie could hear.

Inside the mini-mart, as the man on his knees lapped and his backward cap bobbed like a duck bill against the bottom of Sophie's skirt,

Sophie stirred. She put a hand against the glass, slowly straightened her head on her neck with her other hand. Then she turned toward Natalie and opened her eyes.

And Natalie saw. "Sophie, no," she whispered.

The tears she'd glimpsed, glinting unmistakably in the new daylight, slipped down Sophie's cheeks. Just as Sophie reached down, took cap-guy's head in her hands and thighs, and gave a single, savage twist.

Before he'd even hit the floor, Sophie dropped down on him.

## Still Miss
## Someone

"I'm just getting some air," Benny called from the condo's tiny living room into the tinier bathroom, and stepped out the sliding screen door into the sea wind. For a while, he just stood there, blinking; Jess insisted on closing the curtains when they were indoors, though he remained unclear whether that was to stay hidden or just another Jess-privacy thing. Squinting into the sinking sun while his skin warmed from its air-conditioning coma and started to tingle, he slid a hand into his pocket to check for his cell phone. Then he glanced behind him to make sure Jess wasn't watching, felt ridiculous, and started across the street toward the tilting pier terraced over the scatter of weeds and cracked, colorless shells that passed for beach in Ocean Town, Maryland.

The sun still hung above the horizon, and the pier's splintery wooden railing retained the afternoon heat when Benny leaned on it, but already, the beach had emptied. There was no sandbar along this stretch—the sandbar was for summer people—and no protective harbor, and waves pounded at the shore like fists on a door. People didn't so much swim here as step in, get knocked down, struggle back up laughing less than they expected, and stagger out. In a few hours, the town teens would arrive with whatever beer they'd managed to scavenge, and they'd huddle in whatever protection the weeds offered and get what they could from one another.

Even across the street and over the thud of the waves, he could hear both of the babies crying back in the condo. As soon as she had them swaddled, Jess would be calling for him, because he turned out to have a surprising knack for quieting them. Surprising to him, not her, as far as he could tell.

"Why do you think I brought you?" she often asked when he had them curled on his chest like kittens, sleeping soundly.

And he'd smile, as if he loved the question, instead of simply the sound of her voice aimed in his direction.

He should call right now, he knew. While Jess still had her hands full. Clearly, there was something back in Charlotte Jess needed to forget. He'd never press her on it, had no desire to learn more unless she wanted him to. But that didn't mean *he* had to forget. Did it?

Still, he lingered against the railing, feeling the grit on the slats under his feet, letting the sunlight slip over and into him. He closed his eyes, and the wind kicked up and flung bits of sand against his arms and cheeks like rice. As if the wedding were still going on five weeks later. Not that there'd been a wedding. But there could be, he was almost sure, now. Pretty much any time he wanted. Why would she say no?

Opening his eyes, Benny glanced sideways toward town. Every single night at just about this hour—the edge of evening, almost the exact moment the beach users and retirees and single moms with their strollers *abandoned* the pier, taking their pockets full of possible change with them—the homeless materialized under the awnings of just-closed sunglasses shops, or in the alleys between the low, wooden buildings. So many homeless here. There was one skinny guy in particular whom Benny had seen night after night, leaning against the streetlamp that never lit down there past the end of the row of condos, in the empty stretch before the first Coddie stand. Benny had never ventured close enough to get a good look at his face, and the guy mostly just stood or sat there, played a harmonica occasionally, accepted tossed quarters from rare passersby. But the last few nights, he'd taken to waiting until he was sure Benny was looking, and then casually, slowly, lifting his 50-cent straw hat just an inch or so off his head. From what he'd glimpsed, Benny suspected that guy wasn't even eighteen years old. Was actually a kid.

Should that have made Benny nervous? He supposed it should. Instead, he mostly wanted to make the kid a pancake.

Returning his attention to the beach, Benny stared through the weeds, watched the ocean rise yet again and shatter itself on the shore.

Should he have asked Jess to marry him by now? Probably, yep. It was what he'd wanted, for going on ten years. He just wished he knew what it would mean to *her*. And how could it mean anything to her, in fairness? Her daughter—for whom Jess had jettisoned even grief, along with any ambitions she might ever have had for herself—had pawned off not just her own kid but someone else's, then vanished, apparently for good. Benny was still having trouble believing that. He'd known Natalie had a wild streak—hence, the child—but he'd also thought he'd seen more of her mother in her. More stay-and-fight-like-hell. He'd kind of loved her for it, truth be told, and very much hoped she was all right, wherever she was. At least, that's what he hoped whenever he wasn't furious at her.

Whatever she'd done, it was bad enough to drive her mother from her home. Such as that had been. And now, from what Benny could tell, Jess had completely given up sleep. He'd never once caught her with her eyes closed. She didn't twist around in the covers or get up to wander. But those eyes stayed open, like a corpse's. Except for the flash in them, even in the dark.

No wonder she mostly declined to come when he took the boys out for a stroll or to the sand. No wonder she could barely bring herself to speak, except to the children, most of the time.

On the other hand, there'd been moments....

In the five weeks they'd spent on the road, skipping from tiny town to nowhere-place to new tiny town until he'd finally convinced her to hole up here, just for a spell, they'd made love twice. The second time had been during their first night in the Ocean Town condo, a little less than a week ago, and it had surprised her, he knew. The first time, she'd maybe thought she was doing what she had to, or what he expected. But last week, afterward, she had lain on her pillow for a long while, without her glasses, not so much staring at as studying him. *Reading* him, or something. He'd held still, sweating and spent and a little surprised himself, and let her. Watching the sweat on her tiny, strong shoulders, the knots of muscle under the smooth skin like the bottoms of bird wings. The surprising swell of her breasts under the sheet. The near-smile she couldn't quite get off her face, and the ghosts lurking behind her eyes, which she was actually letting him see.

"I think…" she finally said, after a spell of silence that seemed sweeter than usual, if no less sad. "I think I didn't know how much I wanted to do that."

Benny had nodded. Almost afraid to answer. Eventually, he tried, "I didn't know how much I wanted to, either."

And Jess had given him one quick, saw-edged grin. "Really? I knew *that*."

And now—for longer than he'd hoped, long enough to scare him— he'd held off making another advance, to see if she would. To see if she was starting to find him anything more than useful.

He'd been so sure, for a minute there, that she did. Was *still* sure she would. Someday. He'd bet his life on it, after all. Given up his restaurant

**131**

and his Charlotte world, which was far and away the best he'd ever had until now.

"Benny?" her voice called through the screen window.

Out past the breakers, a whole seagull flock swarmed down on two pelicans bobbing in the slate-gray swells. Benny watched, listened to them all squawking and screaming, until one of the pelicans rose on its long legs, as though preparing to run, and then got knocked sideways by the seagull that stole whatever it was trying to gulp from its mouth. Jess didn't need him yet, she knew. That was her preliminary call. He had a little longer to stand and watch the world's last free things scrounge for scraps.

It amazed him, really. What he'd done, what his life had suddenly become. It also scared him. The whole relationship made so little sense. *He* was the one who'd been to college. At Penn, for God's sake. He'd lived in a hostel on a Greek isle, and scuba-dived with big-eyed emperors and unicorn fish on Palau. He'd had several lovers, and a long, sweet affair with a woman from Nova Scotia whom he didn't love but loved being with, and who'd only stopped coming to the States for her museum work a few years ago. He'd owned two Waffle Houses, and kept both thriving, and made lifelong friends in each. Jess, on the other hand, had nursed a husband she'd known only a few years into his grave, lived in a trailer, worked for more than two nearly friendless decades at a Walgreens, raised one wild daughter, and never left the Eastern seaboard.

And yet. Being with her, traveling with her—*loving* her—turned out to be like living by the ocean: endlessly fascinating. Life affirming, even. And guaranteed to make him feel small. And alone.

And now he'd missed his opportunity to make his phone call, damn it. The condo door had opened. He could feel her back there. The rush of her, *force* of her. Engulfing him.

"Benny? Can you come do your thing?"

He turned, and there she was. Skirt whipping around her knees, shapeless blouse flapping like a luffing sail. Eyes remote as a marlin's, but locked on him. Just maybe loving him, after all. Down the block, the harmonica-kid let loose a single, long note. A hungry seagull-cry. Abruptly, helplessly, Benny broke into a grin. That guy didn't know it, but he'd be getting a pancake supper, cooked up special on the hotplate in the condo.

And Jess. Well. She'd be getting him.

He'd call Charlotte later. Tomorrow, maybe. Just to check on everyone. When Jess finally fell asleep, or took a shower, and wouldn't notice. Though for the life of him, he couldn't think why she'd actually mind.

## See That Twinkle
## in Your Eye

Natalie hadn't expected to sleep at all, and woke to the whirl of red lights through the drawn curtains and the sound of water running. For a moment, the lights mesmerized her, set her nestling deeper into the sheets. They'd been a regular occurrence at her mother's trailer park, after all, her childhood equivalent of a hearth fire. Natalie started to sigh, and the present crashed down on her. She froze, resisting the urge to leap up, throw Sophie over her shoulder, and dive out the bathroom window. She also had to resist a simultaneous compulsion to go straight out the door of this room, cross the street, and drop down on her knees next to the husk Sophie had left of the guy in the green corduroy cap—who'd played a mean air guitar, from what Natalie had seen—and beg his forgiveness.

She could do that right now. Kneel in his blood—not that Sophie had left much—and face what they'd done. And let herself weep.

*And then eat a cop or three?*

She started to shudder, and froze again, watching the lights whip over the walls. Processing the sound. The sound of water. Running.

In an instant she was up and across the room, throwing open the door to the bathroom, ripping back the shower curtain.

"Jesus Christ," Sophie snapped, in Sophie sing-song. "You're stealing my warm."

At first, Natalie just stared, while Sophie went on blithely soaping herself. And humming. All over her torso and legs, she had ugly black and red scrapes and bruises, some of them still studded with road-grit. On her left breast, just above the aureole, a massive blue welt had formed and seemed to hover like a thundercloud. And straight across her neck, the jagged rips Natalie's teeth had left had almost closed, creating a second, leering mouth. Jack-o'-lantern mouth.

"If you don't close that curtain, I'm going all-Archie all night on your ass."

Without even shedding her nightshirt, Natalie leapt into the shower, threw her arms around her oldest friend, and let loose the sobs that had been building for weeks.

The force of them staggered Sophie, almost set them both slipping into the tub. And that made Sophie laugh. It was the same full-belly laugh that had served as soundtrack to most of Natalie's life. She clung tight to her best friend's neck.

"There, now," Sophie said, in a voice she'd almost never let Natalie hear. The voice she must have used with her Roo, when they were alone. When it was late at night, and neither of them could sleep.

"You're here," Natalie gurgled.

"Of course I'm here."

"You're *you*."

"Who else would I be?"

Sophie just kept laughing while Natalie raised a shaky finger and laid it against the scabby, bumpy welts along Sophie's neck. Right where she'd bit through it, less than 24 hours ago. Still sobbing, but more gently, she lifted her finger away and laid her cheek there instead.

Sophie's hands patted her back. The fingers strong, all of them seemingly working. Sophie started to sing, at lullaby volume. *Some Godawful Carpenters song, now? No—Carly Simon?* Through her tears and the rivers of shower water sliding down and between them, Natalie felt a smile spread over her face. Sophie's hands flowed up and down her back. So gentle. That awful song, about it being too late, almost soothing in Sophie's voice. Her breasts bumping against Natale's through the sopping nightshirt. Natalie felt her smile widen, and she nuzzled deeper into the hollow of Sophie's neck as those fingers glided down her spine again. And kept going. Past her waist, pulling up the nightshirt. Sophie's lips against her forehead. Lingering. Then her hands grabbing, the force of the grip stunning. The butt-slap that followed afterward feather-light, as Sophie pushed harder against her.

**136**

Jerking away, almost crashing over the rim of the tub, Natalie wrenched free and banged backwards into the sink and stood in the center of the bathroom floor, dripping, shivering hard as the air hit her, tingling in ways she didn't want to think about. Also, she was furious. "What the *fuck* are you doing?" She grabbed a towel off the rack, ran it savagely through her hair. If she rubbed hard enough, maybe the friction would spark, light her on fire. Then maybe she'd be warm.

Smiling, humming, Sophie shut off the water and stepped out of the shower. She was dripping everywhere. Bruised, pale, perfect. Radiant. She looked radiant. "I don't know," she said. "Um. Whatever I want?" Then she started singing again.

"Seriously?" Natalie said, as Sophie toweled off, starting to shiver, too. Eating made you glow, apparently, and maybe made you horny. But not warm. Which meant they would never again be warm. "You're going to hum *that* song? 'Something inside…'"

"Died," Sophie chirped. "And I absolutely *can* take it. Oh, hon."

Natalie had sagged to the toilet seat. The more she tried not to think—about Eddie, her mom in her trailer, the fact that she'd killed Sophie, the fact that Sophie had killed—the more thoughts roared through her.

Wrapped in two towels, Sophie knelt. Her touch on Natalie's cheek was gentle, now. Helplessly, Natalie leaned into it, let her eyes close. So familiar, that touch. So Sophie. Except for the smell. Sophie didn't smell like RC and Moon Pies anymore.

"Oh, Nat," Sophie said. "You are just not even going to believe how good this feels."

Natalie opened her eyes, stared into Sophie's. "Killing someone, you mean? Taking someone's life?"

"Eating. Being fed." Jumping up, Sophie did a ridiculous pirouette and little cross-toed leap.

"I remember eating," Natalie hissed.

Sophie shook her head. "It's not like that. It's…like you always wanted chicken-and-waffle to taste, only it never does? Like…like eating a whole plateful of *you*."

"Well, that just sounds fantastic. I wish I could take my arm off and devour it right now."

"No…" Sophie sighed, rolling her eyes. Twirling again, as if she were a five-year-old. As if she just couldn't help it. "It's…I don't know. Like a super-cold water fountain on the hottest, hottest day. Like tasting everything again. Yeah. That's it. Like *tasting* again. Like…"

"Living," Natalie whispered, and Sophie stopped. Turned. The smile still all over her face. That was the worst part.

"That's exactly it," Sophie said. "It tastes like living." Only then did she seem to notice the red lights still playing over the carpet and walls out there. "Wait a second." She had stopped prancing about, at least, and was staring into the other room. Her eyes tracked the lights like a cat's. "Are you telling me…" She skipped out of the bathroom, shedding her towel as she reached for a T-shirt, moved to the curtains, and peered out. For a long moment, she stayed still by the window.

*Reality time*, Natalie thought. *Time to remember what eating* really *means, now, no matter how it feels.*

Then Sophie turned around. Her smile, if anything, had gone wider. And even in the shadowy dark, her eyes twinkled. "Are those *our* lights?" She gestured over her shoulder out the window. Toward the dead man she'd left there.

"If you're asking, is that the exact spot where you killed a man and drank his blood twelve hours or so ago, yes."

Sophie threw her head back and laughed. Bobbed up on her heels and came down again. "That was your escape plan? Sprint for the hotel across the street and hope no one sees?"

"Well, making a mad dash to nowhere in particular with the rag doll from hell in the passenger seat didn't seem much better." Natalie heard the snarl in her own voice. Didn't care. "Also, I was tired."

"I understand." Easing around the bed, Sophie glided back across the carpet, smile still glinting. Openly provocative. "You *had* just done some killing of your own, after all. Ms. Holier-than-Thou Nat Queen Cold." And she ran a hand over the bumps on her neck.

The electric tingle in Natalie's skin, that had never quieted from the second she'd awoken, intensified again. And changed. Again. It was warning her, now. "True," she said, and stood. Crouching, just in case. Her nightshirt glued itself to her skin, sealing the cold against her. She peeled it off, stood naked in front of Sophie, who stopped in the shadows five feet away.

She couldn't read her friend's expression. Had no idea what her own was. Felt dizzy, barely able to keep up with it all. Since when, she wondered, had the whole world become a bucking bull? Then she wondered when it had ever been anything else?

"It must have been so hard," Sophie said, stunning Natalie to absolute stillness. This voice barely even sounded like Sophie's at all. It was too gentle.

"Stay there," Natalie managed.

"Last night, I mean. When you thought you'd killed me. When you saw what I'd done. God, Nat. You must have been so lonely."

"I think I still am."

"How'd you even get me up here? I don't remember any of it. Did I walk?"

"Kind of."

"Thank you," Sophie whispered. Her eyes pinning Natalie in place. She was positioned perfectly. There was no way out of this room except through her.

And then, just like that, Sophie laughed and sat down on the bed, leaning back to let the red lights play over her arms, slide down her shirt. "Look," she giggled. "It's like all the little globules I missed last night. And they want to join their friends. Poor little guys. Do you want to come in?" Tilting her head, still cooing, Sophie gave her upper arm a long, soft lick.

Moving fast to get out of the bathroom, Natalie went to her duffle bag and threw on jeans and a shirt. She kept her back to Sophie and tried to get a grip on her thoughts. *Little globules. Poor little guys.* That was Sophie-thinking, all right. And the licking wasn't so different than a thousand other Sophie actions over the course of the last twenty years. Maybe not different at all.  And yet...

She turned and found Sophie staring at her again.

"Natalie," she said, "stop judging me."

"I'm not judging you, Sophie. I don't have any right. I don't even—"

"You knew we had to do it. Sooner or later. You knew there wasn't going to be a choice about that."

"I know. I do know. I just..."

"You're wondering where the remorse is. Right?"

More than anything, Natalie wanted to move to the bed, take Sophie's hand, sit beside her. Lay her head against her shoulder. But she didn't dare. Or maybe just couldn't. Fear. Friendship. Desire. Regret. Remorse. Loneliness. Longing. Hunger. Terror. It was getting so hard to tell the difference between any of those things. If she'd ever been able to. If anyone really could.

"You do have to remember, hon." Sophie's voice had that teasing edge again. Like a tickle. A ruthless one."I was dead at the time."

Once more, Natalie felt a sob rise, and it burst from her mouth like a cough. No tears attached. An emotional dry-heave.

"Well, I'm alive now," Sophie said, and rose. Arms out. The pull of her—whatever its source—absolutely irresistible. "And I'm so, so glad you're here with me. There is no one on this Earth—except my son—I'd rather be here with. Does that help? At all?"

Inside Natalie, something lifted. Or melted away. Or gave up. She stood, too. Tried to smile. "I don't know. And you know what? Right now, I don't care." She stepped into Sophie's embrace—to hug her, to get hugged back—and stiffened again.

Because Sophie had stiffened. Which meant she'd heard it, too.

"Was that a *knock*?"

For a few seconds—just long enough for Natalie to believe she hadn't heard it, after all—there was nothing. Then it came again. More scratch than knock. But too rhythmic to be anything else.

Sophie grabbed her pants and backed toward the bathroom, eyes flashing everywhere. "Is there a window in there? Shit, it's too small. Where's the gun? Natalie, did you bring up that guy's damn gun? The one that shot you?" She kept edging away. Making her new mewling sounds.

Natalie shook her head, trying to clear it. To her surprise, that seemed to work. She watched her friend. "Let me get this straight. You let me all but rip your head off. You ate a guy. But you're scared of the cops?"

Blinking, as though Natalie had thrown water on her, Sophie stopped mewling. But she still just stood there, clutching her jeans to her chest. "You know what, Natalie? I don't know what I am."

"You really *are* like a Lick Em Stick," Natalie snapped. "Different depending on whatever you're being dipped in."

"That's..." She trembled in place, holding the doorframe with both hands. "That's the most *me* thing you've ever said."

"That's why I said it," said Natalie. "Put your pants on. Get ready to run."

The scratching came again. More insistent.

Natalie moved silently to the door, She pursed her lips, blew air through them. An old habit. A good one, though. She put her arms to either side of the frame, steeled herself. Then she leaned forward and peered through the fish-eye.

"Oh, shit," she said.

"Natalie. Are we running?"

"Too late," she muttered. She opened the door and let the Whistler in.

### Traveling Night and Day
### Running All the Way

The tapping at her door came just at dusk, and rattled Wanda out of a dream. In the dream, she'd finally realized what it was she'd always forgotten in her mint juleps—*powdered* sugar, for God's sake—and she woke up giggling like a schoolgirl. Wanda had never made a mint julep in her life. She hadn't even *seen* one since her mother had passed, and that was what, 40 years ago, now? 42?

The second set of taps got her eyes open. She'd been lying on top of the sheets on her bed, with her shoulder wedged against the aluminum siding of her trailer wall, and through that, she could still feel the remnants of the day's heat. Funny things, her dreams. Especially these days. Full of mint juleps and railroad tracks and Ferris wheels and crocheted handbags, but almost no people whatsoever. Which shouldn't have surprised her. Now that her hips hurt her too much to allow her to continue volunteering at the elementary down Sardis, and her daughter's calls had dwindled to one a month, and her friend Emmy's family had moved her north so she could die among them, and Jess had gone, who was there to dream about?

The third barrage bowed the door out of its frame, almost drove it off its hinges, and shadows bubbled around the corners and spread across her warping floor like floodwater. Wanda blinked and pulled herself up.

"Sorry," she called. Her voice rasped, so she took a swallow of the lemon-water she kept by her bed. It tasted lukewarm, too thick, like vegetable oil. She tried calling again. "I thought I'd dreamed you."

Whoever was out there didn't respond. That annoyed Wanda. A simple *"Sorry to disturb you"* or *"No problem"* would have made her feel less pressured, less aware of how long it now took her to get centered over her hips and navigate the eight long steps to the door. That was the thing other people never seemed to understand: the only real problem with getting old was everyone else. When you were on your own—or with someone like Jess, who didn't ask for anything, didn't chatter, just *stayed*—you were still just you.

"Almost there," she called again, and opened the door.

Her surprise showed, and she knew it, and it embarrassed her. At least the evening shadows probably hid her blush.

"That's..." she said, almost fast enough to cover her confusion, while the woman out there just stood with one high-heeled sandal on the trailer's bottom step, eyes high, curly black-and-gray hair perfect under her green bonnet, skin dark and shining and clean as a Cola. "That's a beautiful dress."

And it was. Strange, maybe, but a lovely, glittering green with overlapping leaves that caught the new moonlight and flowed down the woman's substantial body like Spanish moss. Or scales. Wanda's mother might have called it a Visiting Dress. Not that her mother had ever owned such a thing, or had any places she could Visit, except to clean them. But she liked using phrases like that, anyway.

One thing was certain: her mother would never have worn a Visiting Dress to a trailer park. Wanda edged forward into her doorway to get a closer look at the newcomer.

She was older than Wanda had first thought. That is, she *might* have been older. With her face in shadow, Wanda found it hard to tell. She half-wondered if she were still dreaming. Around them, the trailer park had gone uncharacteristically still. Mostly, Wanda heard cicadas. Mutterings and canned laughter from a few TVs.

"Evening, ma'am," the woman said, with a gentleness that erased the ferocity of that last knock from Wanda's mind.

*No, not gentleness*, Wanda thought. *Caution. The caution of a lifelong Southerner.* The realization made Wanda sad. And also, though she hated to admit it, put her at ease.

"Well. Good evening to you."

"Another hot one." The woman took a neatly folded handkerchief from her shiny, green handbag and patted her brow with it, the way actors did. From what Wanda could see, there was no sweat on this woman's forehead, or dust either. In truth, she looked as though she'd never been outside at all, was in fact standing onstage right this minute.

There was a glamour to her, no question. Wanda felt herself straighten, smooth her handmade knit pull-over, as though smoothing it would restore its shape or hide the dangles of loose thread. "It is, at that." She wasn't sure why she was smiling. The smile felt good, though. "Can I help you?"

The woman met her eyes only briefly. "Well, you just might. I'd sure appreciate it. I saw an ad about a double-wide. Vacant and furnished. I was just wondering..." And she glanced—carefully, furtively—toward Jess's trailer.

Wanda liked this woman. She liked her glamour, and also the way she played her part, almost overplayed. It couldn't have been a part she'd chosen, if she'd wound up here. But her disappointments weren't stopping her from doing what was necessary. Jess would have liked her, too. For the first time since Wanda had woken up—a good ten minutes longer than usual, in other words—she thought of her daughter, a lawyer in Connecticut a thousand miles away. The last time Jennie had come, with her new boyfriend, she'd stayed in a hotel over by Southpark Mall. She'd insisted Wanda come stay with them, had even got her a suite. Wanda had felt so ashamed that she'd made Jess come stay in the suite with her. Almost three years ago, now. Somehow, when Jess had been here,

Connecticut hadn't seemed so very far away. Or the weeks between phone calls quite so long. Or quite so hurtful.

And now, this woman had come. To buy Jess's trailer. Which would make it not Jess's, anymore. Which would mean Jess really wasn't coming back. Jess hadn't called either, Wanda realized. The realization surprised her. And it stung.

And so she squared her shoulders, the way Jess had taught her. Fixed her smile right where it was. "Well," she said. "Would you like a Cola? Beer?"

The woman smiled back.

Five minutes later, Wanda was fumbling with the keys at Jess's lock, while the woman waited silently behind her. From three berths down, a stereo blared suddenly. The new family, the stringy mom and the dad in the cap and the two teenagers with dirt bikes and skin that looked too hairy, too dirty even for boys' skin; collectively, they reminded Wanda of possums, skulking and dirty and dead-eyed. The music they played was mostly roaring, like the buzzing thunder from a race car track.

"Sorry," Wanda said over her shoulder, pushing open Jess's door. "They're new. We've talked to the manager, but…" She'd turned as she spoke, only to find the woman right on top of her. Before Wanda could even grunt her surprise, the woman was past, bumping her out of the way with her hip.

But once inside, she just stood. Right in the middle of the trailer. *Like an animal*, Wanda thought. *Like some stalking cat.*

Or, she reproached herself. Like a proud woman who'd landed hard, and had nowhere else to go. And was trying to come to terms with it.

And suddenly, Wanda realized how much she wanted this woman here. Or someone, anyway. She stepped into the trailer and pulled the door closed, shutting out the early-evening moonlight and at least a little of the racket. In the gloom, the woman seemed to swell, gathering the shadows to her like a rising ocean swell and then rolling across the little space, from countertop to bed-berth to the walls, where the whiter spaces marked the places Jess's pictures of Natalie had hung.

"Don't you want some light?" Wanda snapped the switch.

The woman was pulling open drawers, peering into the cabinets over the sink, but now she stopped. Or, she'd already stopped, her head cocked and her wide, proud face expressionless. "Clean as a hotel," the woman said. "You'd never know someone had actually lived here."

"Well, Jess was like that. She lived light. Fought hard, lived light."

"No fool, she," the woman said, with a wistfulness that surprised Wanda.

"She was my best friend." The tears welled in Wanda's eyes, and made her feel even more pathetic than she usually did.

*Best friend. Who hadn't called. And wasn't coming back. Ever. Ever. Ever.*

"Some nights," she said, mostly to herself, letting the bitterness come, "I still come in here and turn on the radio. To the baseball.

I don't even understand baseball; I never know who's playing. But Jess loved it, and I got so used to that sound, you know? If it weren't for her stupid daughter…"

The woman twitched in place, then somehow went even more still. As though she'd turned to stone. As if she wasn't even breathing.

"Her daughter turned out even stupider than *my* daughter."

"But probably not quite as stupid as *my* boy," the woman said, her voice so low it could have been purring, or growling. She turned around, and the smile on her face was kind, sad, but private, too. Perfect. A loneliness shared, like a wave across a backyard fence. She'd be the ideal neighbor, Wanda decided.

"So do you like it? The trailer? I could help you—"

"There's not a single picture." The woman gazed around once more. "Not one thing to suggest where she's gone. I wonder where she went."

"Me, too."

"That's too bad. That's…" And there it was again. That stillness, as though she'd just winked out of her body for a moment, then back into it. "I'm just wondering…how will I know where to send the money, when I buy this place? She must have told you that."

"Not me. My son-in-law's cousin. He's a really big realtor."

"Well, now," the woman said, and her face blossomed into an even more delightful grin. As if they'd just shared the naughtiest little secret. "Perhaps we should phone him."

"Ma'am," said Wanda, grinning right back, "perhaps we should."

And then, startling even herself, she took the woman's chilly, dry arm with her own and led her back out into the night. She felt herself slow as the air slid, so soft, along the hairs of her arm. So much cooler, already, although the coolness seemed mostly to flow from the woman herself. Wanda felt a pride she knew was absurd about all this, about walking arm-in-arm back to her trailer with her new, black friend. She'd never had a black friend.

"I do love it here," she said, with no idea why she was crying, now.

"I can see why," said the woman, with no inflection whatsoever.

The rest went quickly, too quickly. The woman refused a second beer, for the first time seemed a touch impatient as Wanda fumbled in the flaps of her address book for the scrap of paper with the realtor's number. But then, this woman might have nowhere else to go. Might want to get everything arranged so she had somewhere to stay. She could be living here by the end of the week.

Moments later, the woman was out the door, starting down the path, glancing just once toward the new family's trailer, which was positively shuddering on its axles as the drums and guitars and growling voices rumbled. Wanda watched as she stopped, just a few feet away, and went rigid once more. Moonlight caught in the scales of her dress, but disappeared into her skin as though sinking in a silent, black lake.

One final time, the woman turned, glancing around her. But there was no one around. No one to see.

"Ma'am," she said, and stepped back in Wanda's direction. Slowly. Her eyes settling on Wanda's, now. Locking in.

"Yes?" said Wanda, swaying.

"You've been such a help already. I hate to impose. But I wonder if I could trouble you for just one more thing...."

She'd reached the step again, was gazing up at Wanda.

"Anything," Wanda murmured.

"It's just…" said the woman. "Well, this is so embarrassing. But I've been out looking all day, every day, for weeks on end. I'd just about given up when I saw this place. And I really do hate to ask. But you've been so kind." And there it was again. That delightful, vaguely wicked smile.

"Just tell me what you need," said Wanda.

"Well. Ma'am. I just wondered if you had anything to eat."

**Is You Is**

*He'd seen the Caution tape, of course he had, taken note of the police cars blocking off either entrance to the gas station. But not until he heard the sweet snick of the deadbolt sliding back did it occur to him what might have happened. The realization alone almost staggered him, and then came a surprising burst of heat, of actual warmth, that raced up his arms and burrowed into his flannel shirt and up under the brim of his sombrero. I'm* blushing, *he thought, and nearly laughed as he began to tremble. He saw her feet, his Destiny's beautiful, pale, bare feet, and he started to look up and realized he couldn't, not yet. He was downright overcome. And the heat bubbling up in him had brought images with it, a freckle-faced brunette in one sandal with magnolias on its straps disappearing into the boughs of a weeping willow, in sun so blinding…*

*My God, he thought, was that* memory? From before? *He'd almost forgotten there* was *a before. Whatever it was, it brought with it a more familiar sadness, hollow and cavernous. All these wasted years with Mother.*

**153**

*All the empty decades, really believing the way it had become was the only way it could be. To his amazement, he felt himself smile, the smile like sun—like the memory of sun—burning the years away in a single, glorious blast. He started to lift his hand to his hat, his face to his Destiny's, and froze.*

*The heat wasn't coming from inside him. Never had been. It was coming from her. He could see it, dancing like St. Elmo's Fire along the fine, dark hairs of her arms.*

*"But then, you haven't…" He couldn't even make himself complete the sentence. The disappointment hammered him, even as he slipped inside, noting how she scuttled back. He closed the door, held on to the knob to keep himself steady.*

*Too soon. He'd come too soon. Gotten impatient. It was almost funny, after so many decades of waiting, of not even waiting, just drifting. He tried again to lift his gaze, found he couldn't. At least the ache that seized him now was actually seizing him, twisting down his throat like a funnel cloud and whipping everything around in there. He could never use this feeling to Whistle. The Whistle came from the cavern where his soul had been. And it Whistled because it was empty.*

*Which meant it wasn't empty, now. Wasn't empty. His mood turned again, and he wanted to throw his hands in the air or, better still, around his Destiny, even though she couldn't be his yet. In fact, he thought he'd do precisely that, and this time did raise his eyes, just in time to glimpse the stem of the floor lamp hurtling toward his head. He grabbed, twisted, hurled the lamp and the girl still clutching the other end across the room into the wall. The slam shook* the whole room, should have shattered the girl to pieces. But she landed on her feet, fists up and poised, eyes dead on him.

The Other One, the Whistler realized. His Destiny's friend. And he knew, abruptly, that he wasn't early after all. Whatever was rocketing around inside him erupted from his mouth in a whoop of what he really thought must be joy. It kept coming, too, swept him up completely, the anguish of moments before obliterated, the rush of it so ferociously fast, terrifying and marvelous, like a plunge over a falls, a childhood dream of a fairground ride. Like actual time passing.

"I thought…" he said, when he felt he could speak. "When you opened the door…I actually thought you hadn't finished."

He registered the twitch in the Other One's stare, the sudden dart of her eyes toward his Destiny's. His Destiny, right behind him. Not three feet away. He would turn, soon. And there she would be. But not yet. He would hold this moment just a little longer. Savoring.

"What?" the Other One hissed.

She was beautiful, too, in her way. Not Strong like his Destiny. But luminous, in a way he hadn't realized. Round and vibrant. A morning sun to his Destiny's full moon. Except for the eyes, which were hard, hard, now. Mother's eyes. Almost. Whistler smiled at her anyway. Why wouldn't he? She wouldn't be with them long.

"When I first saw you," he explained, "I had this silly thought. Like maybe you'd decided not to."

This time, he not only registered the Other One's blink, but understood it.

*My God, he thought. She* hadn't known. *Hadn't realized.* Still *didn't know. The realization thrilled him. Aroused him. He'd been sure Mother must have said something that night outside the Waffle House. The fact that she hadn't… that she'd proven, once again, so much crueler than even he'd given her credit for…*

*Again, he sensed the movement in the air, but for once—somehow—he moved too late. The first blow, to his temple, drove him to his knees. The second shattered his cheekbone and crumpled him backward over himself. And then both women were on him.*

*It took one painful shake to clear his head, would have required barely a twitch to shuck himself of these clawing hands and clumsy, bumping knees, but he hesitated. The pain, first of all, was downright invigorating, the worst he'd felt in years. But more importantly, this was his Destiny astride him. Her thighs locked around his chest, her fingernails raking his already-battered face. Her wet, dirt-dark hair dangling down, right over his lips. If he wanted, he could slurp her in, like spaghetti. So savage in her fury, she was, and yet so marvelously silent. A force of nature. He'd chosen well. Even Mother had known it. Which is why she'd fled.*

*As though sensing his thoughts, his Destiny stopped raking, balled her fist, and punched him right in the shattered place, so that his hips arched against the Other One, who had somehow managed to pin his legs, and he howled, twisted hard, and his Destiny leapt to her feet and out of his reach. For a long moment, he just lay there, legs pinned to the floor, hand to his face, snarl in his throat and an agonizing smile on his lips. He let his gaze flick, just for a* moment, away from his Destiny to the Other One, and she jumped away, too, as though from an electrified fence, and stood beside her friend.

"Get up," the Other One commanded, as if she had anything to say about it whatsoever. She was undeniably intoxicating, too. In a more familiar, secretly fearful sort of way.

"Stay down," snapped his Destiny. Her voice full of doubt, and infinitely stronger. Even unFinished, and desperately hungry. Because she clearly was hungry. He'd been right all along. The Other One had Finished. But not this one. The power of her stunned him. Filled him with yearnings he'd Whistled instead of truly feeling for so long that he'd forgotten living things actually felt them. God, but he wanted her.

"How about we compromise?" he purred, and slithered to his knees. Hands out. A classical pose. Poet to his Beatrice. Painter to his muse. He'd forgotten the stabbing pain in his face, or else it was already fading. His Destiny took a step back. So wise. And yet her eyes did not so much as blink, let alone leave his face.

"How'd you even find us?" the Other One whined.

As always, the Whistler felt a certain pride at such questions, and even more in answering them. If not for the agony now spreading into his jaw, he would have grinned. "Tweetybirds," he said.

"Shit, Nat, you knocked him senseless."

It was the panic in the Other One's voice, not her pathetic attempt at humor, that did indeed trigger the Whistler's grin, despite the pain it shot through his mouth. "Sorry. My Tweetybirds." And then, when both women exchanged more baffled looks, "Where, even in the stupid stories, does anyone say someone like me wouldn't be able to use a smartphone?" He rewarded himself with just a glimpse toward his Destiny. She didn't seem to be paying attention. Was staring back and forth from her friend to the floor.

"You mean you...Tweeted?" said the Other One. "You Tweet?"

"I have over 5,000 Followers," said the Whistler. "All I have to do is... Whistle. And they tell me what I want to know. You have been creating some small stir in your wake, you understand."

"What do you mean?" his Destiny whispered.

Even the sound of her breath, without even any voice in it, seemed to bend the Whistler's bones together, set them singing like a musical saw. "What do I mean?" He turned, and ignoring the pain, he smiled again. He couldn't help it. It astonished him to discover how delightful and excruciating courtship turned out to be when it meant something to the courter. He'd forgotten that. Or maybe never known it. Even before. "I mean to have you. And I'll Tweet, and I'll Whistle, and I'll follow over mountains and through the valleys, too —"

"Finished," his Destiny hissed. "What did you mean when you said, finished?"

"Oh." The Whistler's smile widened, which caused his eyes to water. His Destiny, of course, had skipped right past the trivialities. Had, in fact, never bothered with them at all. Was shining her beautiful light right on the essential point. The Other One was, too, he saw now; she simply hadn't been able to face it, yet. Because she wasn't his Destiny.

He floated to his feet. Neither woman protested. Because they already knew *what he was about to tell them? God, this night just kept getting better. And better. And better. "I was just so sure you knew. Surely Mother must have told you. I assumed that's why she kicked me back into the truck and spoke to you that night. Mother's a sporting one, generally."*

*"You're talking about finishing transforming," said his Destiny. "Into you. Aren't you?"*

*"Maturing, I think. That's a better word. And into* you, *not me."*

*"Meaning we're not Finished yet."*

*This is like orgasm, the Whistler thought. That really was the only comparison he could imagine. He held the moment as long as he could. Then let go, with a wracking, riveting shudder that he tried, as much as he could manage, to fashion into a shrug as he gestured with his chin toward the Other One. "She is."*

*After that, he just watched it happen. The glance the girls exchanged, then the second, as the true meaning of what he'd said dawned. Such a* privilege, *he thought. Actually getting to be here to see this. His Destiny's hand lifting, falling back, as the gulf opened between her and her friend. The Other One with her mouth open, already borne away on the current of her own actions, with no oars in her boat, no way back. What stunned him, most of all—what made it even more magical than he could possibly have dreamed—was the* lack *of pleasure he felt, as his Destiny twitched on her feet and her mouth opened and real loneliness, the kind people dread and dream of all their sorry, scrabbling lives, rushed into her for the first time. I'm* sad, *he thought, and really did cock his right foot in the first step of a dance he'd forgotten he knew. If he'd thought it would help, he would have taken her in his arms and just held her.*

For amusement—and because his Destiny kept doing it—the Whistler did eventually look again toward the Other One. He was glad he did, because she was an entirely different flavor of delicious. She had her hands at her heart, and was gulping at the air for no conceivable purpose. But her eyes betrayed her. Oh, yes they did. Where his Destiny was desperate, engulfed, staving off panic by sheer force of will, the Other One looked mostly confused. She was still close enough to having felt, of course, to remember what that felt like. But not close enough actually to feel. Not in the same way. For a moment, the Whistler experienced an echo of something he didn't recognize. Not remorse, surely. But a strange sort of…kinship. Perhaps he could help this one, at least a little, since she was his Destiny's friend. Explain a bit more, if he could find the words. His Destiny would appreciate it if he did. He opened his mouth, but his Destiny spoke first.

"I can go back to my son?"

Son? At first, the Whistler had no idea what she meant, and then he remembered. Yes, he remembered, now. She had indeed babbled something about a child, as he'd lowered her, gently, Hungrily, into the back seat of that car. Had done so again near the end, as he'd held her in his arms, stunned at what he'd somehow managed to do. And perhaps even a third time, right at the moment he undid her.

His Destiny's son.

She was still murmuring. To herself, though only he could answer her questions. "All I have to do is not kill? Not eat? Is that right?"

Stirring abruptly, the Whistler shook his head. "No. No. Stop that. It's—"

"She said the hunger would make us," said his Destiny, and looked up.

"That woman. The one you travel with. She said sooner or later, it would just take over."

If he could only hold her, the Whistler thought. If she could feel his love. But she wouldn't allow it. Not yet. "It makes most," he said, low and purring, his admiration absolutely genuine, the sensations inside him intensifying with every word that passed her dry, sad lips. "Everyone I've ever known. But you... you're so strong. Maybe you could fight it. Meaning, die. Which would be such a waste. So unnecessary. Don't you see..."

And even as he said the words, he realized yet again—and yet again, late—just how intoxicating this whole scene had become. Because he didn't register the gun in his Destiny's hand until she raised it. She'd hit him with that, not five minutes ago, and he hadn't even seen it then.

Her hands were shaking too much for her to shoot him, fortunately. Her emotions running riot, flushing her skin a thousand different shades, as though her veins and arteries had opened inside her, spilled into each other. All those crazy, crushing feelings. Grief, loss, loneliness, fury. Love? Was that love?

"Oh, my Destiny," he cooed, stepping forward. Miscalculating yet again, because by the time he realized the danger, the Other One had ripped the gun out of his Destiny's hands and shot him through the shoulder.

Driven backward, howling, the Whistler barely even felt the second slug explode in his stomach. What he did notice, as he collapsed into a crouch, guts popping out of his belly to flap against his knees—squirmy and too dry, even to him, and so cold—was his Destiny clawing at the Other One's raised arms, screaming in her face.

*Screaming for the Other One to stop. His Destiny. Saving him.*

*"Sophie, fucking STOP!" Tears pouring down her gorgeous, tortured cheeks. Black hair like a shredded cocoon around her. Wings of her about-to-be-born self just unfolding. Still so wet and new.*

*She had the gun, now. And the Other One had dredged up a sob, too, or perhaps could still generate a real one from the dead, drying reservoir of whomever she'd been. She stood there shuddering, staring down at the new rents her best friend had clawed in her arms.*

*Once more, the gun was now leveled at him. With one hand, he pushed at the sludgy weight of his insides, shoving them back into his skin like an old pillow into a case. The pain was perfect, radiating out from his middle and down his arms in all directions. Like heat. Almost.*

*"Tell me again," his Destiny said. Her voice completely steady now.*

*"You are my Destiny," he answered.*

*No reaction whatsoever. "About the Hunger. About how I can choose to ignore it."*

*"Natalie," the Other One mewed, pitifully.*

*His pain all but forgotten—except when he straightened, and his guts twisted together, pressing at the jagged rip in his center—the Whistler offered his gentlest smile. The one he usually saved for the songs that hurt and helped them all so badly. Even him, sometimes. "But you won't. You're my Destiny. You won't be able to. You'll choose me."*

*His Destiny's snarl was savage, terrifying, beautiful to behold. And her words were for herself. "You underestimate me."*

*"Not anymore. My only one. Never again. Which means I know I'm going to have to make you."*

*And before either woman could react, he sprang between them, snatched the framed photograph he'd glimpsed on the nightstand, and was through the door and past the pair of policemen racing up the hotel stairs. And then he was gone.*

## See You Later,
## Alligator

Somehow, her instincts outracing her thoughts, Natalie held herself together just a little longer, as the footsteps on the landing hurtled toward their open doorway and Sophie snatched at her elbow, mewling—or was that giggling? —"Nat, Nat, Nat, we gotta *move*." And sweet God, her instincts were *fast*. It was like a watching a third creature that scythed itself free, flashed out a claw and ripped Sophie's halter top fully off one shoulder, peeling it all the way down the swell of her breast. Another flash, to rip her own T-shirt, this time, from the bottom right up over her crotch. A lightning shake of both of them to get their hair wild, and finally, quick as a flicker, in the instant after the pair of cops had erupted through the door but before they'd processed what they were seeing, a bend-and-tuck of the gun into the back of her pants.

*Female cops*, Natalie noted vaguely. Knowing it wouldn't matter. Then she fell against Sophie, spinning them both toward the door so the newcomers got their first glimpse full blast, and let her scream loose.

"It was *him*," she wailed, completely authentic sobs exploding from her throat, free arm flailing in the direction the Whistler had gone. "It was him, it was him, it was him."

Crawling all over each other in their desperation to respond, the cops stumbled from the room and raced off shouting. Natalie's cries cracked over their heads like a whip. But Natalie wasn't really driving them intentionally. And she couldn't get her shrieking to stop.

"Natalie," Sophie hissed, and Natalie bit down on the insides of her own mouth and locked her teeth together so that the screams became squeals, then grunts, then ground to silence.

"It was him," she said, through a haze of pain-tears. Which were also missing Eddie-tears. And Hunger.

"Yes it was," Sophie murmured.

Gunshots sounded outside, somewhere across the street. All kinds of scurrying. Sirens, too. When Natalie unclenched her jaws, she could feel shreds of her cheeks in her teeth. She shook her whole body like a dog, grabbed Sophie with her glare. "*Now* we move. Grab everything."

Sophie was already in motion. And this time, she was definitely giggling. "We didn't bring anything. Did we? What did we bring?"

"Mostly you. Grab the towels. All of them."

"We're taking a night-dip?"

"I don't want to leave them your blood. Or the guy's, the gas station guy's." Natalie gagged, willfully, to keep from screaming again or having to bite back down. "Just grab everything."

"You're such a *mom*."

"Yes I was," Natalie whispered. And held the wall to keep her feet.

It was such a relief to let Sophie pull her to the doorway, then out into the shadows on the landing. Across the street, people seemed to be racing in all directions, looking everywhere but up here. And why would they look up here? Or ever check this room again? Just a couple girls who got freaked by an intruder and fled, the way girls would.

"Come on," Sophie whispered, voice gleeful, like a little kid playing Ghost in the Graveyard. She pulled Natalie away from the landing toward the back staircase. Natalie was barely lifting her feet, just letting Sophie lead her, and yet the world whipped by so impossibly fast.

"Where's the…" she murmured, but Sophie had already seen it, was hustling them toward the GTO parked across the dirt road that ran along back of the hotel, all but invisible in the shadows of the Georgia pines.

*As if I knew this would happen,* Natalie thought, wondering if intuition was something else she'd gained when she stopped breathing, before remembering the actual reason she'd parked there.

*So that no one would observe her dragging her best friend up the back stairs. Or notice the blood bubbling from Sophie's lips and all down the front of her dress. Or see the smile on Sophie's face.*

"Hey, zombie, let the vampire drive," Sophie chirped, sliding a hand into the front pocket of Natalie's jeans and pulling out the keys. Then she pushed Natalie around toward the passenger side toward the pebbled, pine needle-strewn shoulder. The black and looming woods.

This time, instinct rose out of the ground like a rogue wave, all but swept her away. Would have, if she hadn't clung to the roof of the car as though it were a buoy. Knowing she should let go. Knowing she should run.

Another completely involuntary cry escaped her, compulsed from some elemental center. *Like birdsong,* she thought crazily. *This was the difference between birdsong and singing, at least the way most people sang. All that avian whistling and cheeping wasn't a reaction or an expression but the thing itself,* feeling *itself. For every living thing but us. Poor birds. Poor, frantic, ferocious things.*

Why did she get in the car? She wondered that even as she did it, and she would go on wondering, though her answer stayed the same. *Because I'm not a bird.* Of course, she wasn't a human, either, anymore. Whatever she was, she chose to stay because she could.

And because it was her fucking car. And because it had the radio.

For a long while—for hours, it seemed while they hurtled down a road that never seemed to curve, past peach orchards and solitary, shambling farm houses and the occasional pick-up truck packed with black-clad, juiced-up teens whose eyes flashed in the headlight beams like cats'—she managed to keep her latest anxiety cornered. Or rather, drown it in even more alarming ones. Along with the one impossible, unimaginable, hopeful one. *She is*, the Whistler had said. Meaning that Sophie was. And Natalie *wasn't*?

*Was that right? Was there a possible way out? And if the way involved starving to death—eating herself completely out of existence, from the inside, instead of devouring someone else—could she do that? Did she want to? And if she could...and did...mightn't she let herself see Eddie again? Just once more? When she was absolutely sure it was too late?*

One thing was certain: the Whistler thought she could do it. Or might be able to. She'd seen that he did. And that had scared him. That's why he'd said that last thing, about having to make her. *What did that mean?*

"Sophie..." she murmured, stirring abruptly, half-climbing out of her seat, and Sophie turned. Grinning. Moonlight on her teeth, and in her mouth.

"I didn't even know you had this, Natalie," she said, holding up a tape, waving it in the air. "Did you bring this for me?" Then she jammed the cassette in the deck and cranked the volume.

"Lover of the Bayou?" Those wasp-buzz guitars rattling in the speakers, electrifying the air. Did Sophie even *like* this song? *Do I*, Natalie wondered? Cringing, she pulled her knees to her chest and her hands to her ears. But the buzz penetrated, demanding the lightning shock, pulling it down into the car. Sophie floored the accelerator and threw her head back, eyes all but closed, hips arching up off the seat, free hand flung out her open window to snatch the wind she'd created. She was screaming some Sophie-approximation of the words, exactly the way Sophie would have.

If Sophie would ever have screamed this song. Which she wouldn't. Natalie knew, definitely, that they really were different people, now, Sophie and she. Or, different whatever-they-were. They'd always been, but now dangerously so. Under cover of a grimace, Natalie glanced out her own window, saw gravel flying past, the shadows of the woods lapping right up onto the shoulder. She'd shatter bones on the asphalt when she hit. Maybe. The bones would heal. Or they wouldn't. Either way, the woods would hide her. Then they'd both be free.

She allowed herself one sidelong glimpse of her oldest friend. The person she'd come closest to sharing her life with. But she felt nothing. Felt the threat, and no more. *You're not her*, Natalie whispered to herself, not even sure which of them she meant. It didn't matter.

She slipped her fingers around the door-handle, tensed for the leap, turned, and Sophie grabbed her by the back of the neck and smashed her face-first into the dashboard and unconsciousness.


She woke to weight and warmth pressing down. And also lifting her up. Like a blanket. But wet. A magic carpet, because she was flat on her back, and trees were floating by. She closed her eyes, opened them. Saw trees floating by, as though she were flying. *Was she flying?* Kicking in sudden panic, Natalie sat up too fast and the world tilted over and she keeled sideways and almost tipped off the side of the flat-boat before Sophie yanked her back and pushed her prone again. Blinking back frustration tears, Natalie writhed against the ropes at her ankles and wrists, and then stopped. When she opened her eyes fully, she could feel black bruises pulsing underneath them. She stared upward.

Into trees. Heavy, hulking things, leaning over as the boat drifted beneath, silent and hooded in their leaves and moss like nuns in a convalescent hospital. Their branches stirred in the rain, which filtered through as mist and settled on Natalie's saturated skin, beading rather than penetrating. On one branch, not five feet over her head at the moment she passed, she saw a skink crouch into itself. Saw the skink see her. Beyond the skink, other things watched, skittered upward and away, which made the trees seem less nuns than fairy-tale giants, with worlds in their hair. An owl hooted, and somewhere well away, back in the real world, thunder rumbled.

Once, years and years ago, the summer after Natalie's father died, Sophie's parents had taken them both to Sophie's great aunt's cabin on the Okefenokee for a month, and the old woman had made them low-country boils and filled their stomachs with sausage-flavored shrimp and their evenings with swamp stories. In one, a bobcat ate a skink and lost its balance as a result and fell off its perch and got swallowed whole by an alligator. In the story, that had sounded like justice.

"Whoops," Sophie murmured, as the metal under Natalie bumped, then scraped. Then they were drifting again.

Slowly, this time, head still spinning and the sweat and mist rilling down her forehead into her eyes, Natalie sat up. The ropes sagged from her wrists and slid halfway off. Natalie held them up.

"Were these supposed to restrain me? Are those supposed to be knots?"

Sophie gave both oars a gentle pull and poked at the black, bulging root that had momentarily hooked them. "I don't know from knots. Do you?"

Thunder rolled again, no closer but long and loud. Glancing over the sides of the boat proved unsettling. The water looked smooth as a mirror, inky-black, except where logs and roots rose out of it or ripples materialized for no visible reason and radiated toward them. Looking up, Natalie could see no stars, not even sky, just trees and mist. *Was it even raining? What difference would it make in air this fetid?* To their right, something whooped and flapped.

"Crane," Sophie said.

"How'd you know?"

"I used to come here, remember, every—"

"About me. That I was going to jump out of the car."

Sophie leaned way back on the oars, elbows jutting over the water, almost touching the surface. Natalie could see condensation forming in the down of her arms and the hollow of her throat. Her skin green-hued, thin as birch bark in the low glimmer of glowing green mist that passed for moonlight. She shrugged. "I don't know. Just another thing that happens, I guess, when you've Fed." Then she lowered gaze to Natalie. "Telepathy."

She waited until Natalie pursed her lips and looked away, then burst out laughing.

"Either that or I've known you my whole life. How do you think I knew?"

Sophie's laugh was still her laugh, bubbling all over everything. And for a moment, Natalie let herself love that.

"You knocked me out. *Out*. You bashed my head in."

"You were going to leave me," Sophie said. Her laughter gone. Hair plastered into her cheeks like little cracks. "You were really going to leave me."

The boat bumped again, on the right side, then up in the stern, by Sophie's dangling elbow. Sophie sat up straight, pushed hard. Natalie's eyes never left her face. It floated there in the heavy air, glowing like the luminous moss on the black gum trees all around. Sophie caught her eyes again.

"You were going to leave me, Natalie."

Natalie nodded. She couldn't think what else to do.

"Well, you can't."

They'd drifted into a wide spot in the river, or whatever this was, and the trees cleared, and actual moonlight blazed down, white and hard. It leached the color out of the moss, the leaves, probed the grooves in the roots and driftwood floating everywhere.

"Why are we here, Sophie?"

Sophie wasn't looking at her anymore. She was watching the water. Her answer seemed to come from far away. From the surrounding trees. "It just seemed like somewhere to go. So you couldn't run, and we could figure this out. Where were you even going?"

Natalie shook her head, which hurt. "Hadn't thought that far." She rubbed at the moisture on her wrists and forearms, which wasn't cold, and seemed closer in consistency to oil than water. Around them, the night-swamp stirred and rustled. At least being knocked out had relieved the Hunger for a second. But it was back, now. A cramp with teeth, chewing up her esophagus toward the air. As though it, too, wanted to get free and run.

"Sophie," she said, curling forward, pulling her arms in tight against her sides. "What if I have to? What if we can't be together anymore?"

"We can," said Sophie, and the boat bumped. Without straightening, Natalie glanced sidelong, saw detritus everywhere. Leaves that spun in their own whirlpools, sank away to nowhere, rose again. Roots and long, gnarled logs. That weren't logs, of course. Not all of them.

"Jesus Christ," Natalie whispered, settling tighter into her crouch. "Sophie…"

"You're staying, Natalie," Sophie said, eyes on the water. The things in the water.

"What if I don't want to anymore?" And then Natalie remembered.

The revelation she'd had right before Sophie had jammed her face into the dashboard. The reason she had to run. Fly. *Now*. "Sophie, you don't understand, he's going to—"

At the splash, Natalie half-stood, almost tipped the boat, sat down fast and grabbed the sides and skidded over to the edge, shouting, *"Sophie, no."* She bored her eyes into the exact spot where Sophie had vanished, the center of the ripples that were already somehow stilling themselves, surrendering to the weight of the air, the will of the water. She shot out a hand, saw the alligators to either side of it, and suddenly they were right up against the boat. Two of them, just floating there.

When Sophie surfaced, she did so right between them.

For a long moment, and then another—too many, too long—everything floated, and nothing moved. Natalie was leaning over the side, arm half-extended, paralyzed. All she could see of Sophie was her eyes, the top of her nose, her hair streaming behind her, her dress a shred of lily-pad reshaping and settling as the water lapped into and over it. So small, suddenly. Just Sophie, and nothing more. With a single snap, the alligators could tear her to pieces.

But neither alligator so much as twitched. When Natalie dared a glance toward the one on the left, though, she caught a glimpse of its orange eye, just peeking out through its nictitating lid, like a trailer-park gossip from behind a curtain. A gossip with scales, and teeth. She glanced away just in time to see the alligator on the right bump up against Sophie. Without seeming to move. As if by accident.

"Soph," Natalie whispered, the whisper catching in her mouth, because she knew, or thought she knew, why this had happened. The news the Whistler had delivered—the truth about the way they were now—had devastated Sophie at least as much as it had her. Doomed her, in fact. Not just to her fate. But just maybe to her fate without Natalie. *Because unlike me,* Natalie thought, self-loathing bitter in her mouth, *she'd thought first about her friend, and not herself.* "Oh, Soph. I'm so sorry…"

Then she saw the bubbles around Sophie's mouth. And heard her purring. Unless that was one of the alligators.

"Sophie," Natalie whimpered.

But Sophie didn't move. For the second time, the right-hand alligator nudged up against her. The ridges of its scales bristly up close, like cactus skin. Its bulk seemed to swell as it spread along Sophie's flank, and inside its barely parted jaws, Natalie saw the same, ember-ish orange that lit the eyes, as though everything were alight in there.

Abruptly, the one on the left wriggled, rocking the boat and almost tipping Natalie backward, and when she'd grabbed the sides and got herself straightened, she saw *both* gators touching Sophie. Nuzzled around her, almost locked to her, tidy as puzzle pieces.

Back and forth Natalie stared. Her whole body rigid, tingling. She couldn't take her eyes off the gators. And she didn't want to look at Sophie. Because every time she did, she realized all over again that Sophie was smiling.

Finally, she edged forward on her bench as far as she dared. "Sophie. What the fuck are you doing?"

For the first time since she'd gone over the side, Sophie's mouth cleared the surface. She was smiling, all right. "Swimming," she said.

Natalie closed her eyes, fighting back the nausea, which was also terror, which was also loneliness more terrible than any she'd felt, even in last few weeks. But mostly, this was terror.

"You should come in, Natalie," Sophie said. "The water's fine."

The right-hand alligator lifted its head slightly, so that its teeth floated in the air, half an inch from Sophie's face. Its eye bored into hers.

"Holy shit," Sophie breathed. "Hello."

Around them, the wetness intensified, the rain not new, not even stronger, really, just refocused, like spray from the nozzle of a hose. The alligator lowered its head. The right-hand alligator had vanished. Could have been anywhere by now, under the boat, under Sophie with its jaws wide open.

The remaining alligator seemed to have stretched out flat, almost seeming to sleep. Or pretending to.

"You really won't come in, Nat?"

"You're lucky they're not hungry."

"And they're lucky I'm not," Sophie half-sang, in lullaby-tones.

For the third time, Natalie remembered what she'd realized she knew. She jerked hard on the bench, banged her knees into the boat-bottom.

*Which means I know I'll have to make you.* That's what he said.

"Oh, God," Natalie said, holding on. Then she grabbed for the oars.

"Oh, no you don't," Sophie laughed, edging away from her new companion, grabbing the side. "I swear, I'll pull you down here with me."

"Sophie," Natalie hissed, "you stupid, blind, reckless bitch. He's going for our children."

## Invite Them Over

## Again

Jess had Eddie on her hip—sidelong, so he could feel her laughing, which made him giggle—but Roo had climbed almost out of the sling again, latched half to her hair and half to her shoulder with his wet cheek at her chin. She'd been spinning for five minutes straight, holding the radio as far from her body as she could with her free hand so Roo couldn't try to climb *that*, and when the doorbell rang, she first assumed she'd bumped one of the kid-toys and went on spinning, while tiny hands flung fingerpaint-blotches of color and heat all over her skin, and not-so-tiny voices filled the emptiness with echoes. Smoky cinnamon smells poured from the kitchen, and through the curtains, which she'd let Benny open, the last red streaks of sunset settled over the pier, made it look red and wet, almost new once more.

The second ring stopped her so suddenly that Roo banged his head against her jaw and started to shriek. So Eddie did, too.

Jess ignored them. Held them tight. Stared at the door. "Benny," she said, but of course he couldn't hear her over the racket. She pulled both kids to her breast, held them close. Felt them calm. So quickly, as if she'd cast a spell. As if she still had magic in her, or ever had.

"Benny," she said again. She started to tremble, made herself stop. That spell, at least, she *knew* she still had mastered.

Again, the doorbell rang.

"Honey, could you grab that?" said Benny, leaning half out of the kitchen doorway and doffing his spatula at her like a tap-dancer's cane.

He registered the astonishment in her face, the glare she could feel forming—of course he did; Benny registered if she so much as squinted—and in response, he grinned. That infuriated her even more. He'd been cooking for close to an hour, she realized. Had plastic platters out on the counter, that he'd brought home earlier this afternoon. And she'd missed it. Assumed, so blithely, that he'd keep doing what she'd asked him to, because she knew how he felt about her. As if that was enough. As if that was how relationships ever worked. As if she didn't know better.

"You know who this is, don't you?" she said. Leaning over, she put both children in the bassinet. Neither protested.

"Unless it's the UPS truck with that backyard I ordered for the kids, yeah. It's our guest."

"Benny."

"What? Jess, for Christ's sake. We need to see people sometime. *You* need—"

"I told you. I warned you. I told you."

"Answer the door. Please?"

Instead of moving that way, Jess went into the bedroom and began gathering her things, and the kids' things. Just like that. It wouldn't take long. She never left anything out at the end of any day. So that she'd always be ready, when this day came. Because she'd known it would. It always came.

Except that last time, it had been Joe leaving, not her. And he hadn't needed to pack anything.

Joe. So long since she'd thought about him, except in the way she thought about him all the time, in her dreams, in the shower, during pitching changes in the middle of baseball broadcasts. He just kind of hovered in the back of her mind, alongside the peach trees from her parents' tiny backyard in Kentucky, and the 10th-grade Chem teacher with the steel-wool curls who'd told her she really might want to stick with this, and cars she'd owned. He'd been learning to tango, ostensibly to please her, though she was a jitterbugger, and he liked taking pictures and fancied himself an artist with potential he'd never quite exploited, and he liked his hot dogs with too much relish and his sex a little straight. And that was all she'd managed to keep of the man she'd married. Almost all she'd known. Maybe all there was, really. He hadn't had time or experience or disappointment enough to become more.

Although he'd had dying. And he'd been plenty disappointed about that.

In the kitchen, she heard Benny drop his spatula. "Just a minute," she heard him say to the front door, instead of opening it. That was something, anyway. More than Joe ever had, Benny paid attention to what she needed, or maybe she'd gotten better at expressing it. He was in the bedroom with her, now. She expected him to start an argument. Instead, he waited for her to turn around. Eventually—to her own surprise—she did.

And there he was, in his paisley cooking apron and egg-stained wife-beater. Salt-and-pepper hairs sticking out all over, but soft, somehow. Like a well-used loofa. Just add water.

"You've told me nothing, Jess. You told me we needed to lay low. We've laid. You said it'd just be you and me." Right on cue, Roo squawked. And Benny…Benny smiled. "And it is," he said.

And Jess realized she loved him. Or could love him. Really could, one day. Soon. "I said—"

"What you *didn't* say was 'Benny, we need to drop off the face of the Earth.' Or, 'Benny, if you decide to give even one homeless kid one of your legendary homeless-kid pancake suppers, even once, I'm leaving you.' Or, 'Benny, stop being you. I just need some chest hair to sleep on.'" And again, he smiled.

If there hadn't been someone at the door, Jess would have shown him exactly what she'd discovered she thought of his chest hair. She didn't think he would have minded. Neither would she.

"Benny, goddamnit."

"I know," he said.

"No, you don't."

And now her daughter's face rose between them, right up out of the floorboards. Looking the way it had on that last night, hovering over Jess in the trailer. But this time, instead of flooding Jess with anger, the sight paralyzed her with guilt. *Because I failed her,* she realized. *Utterly. Completely. In a way Joe would never have let me.* She'd dropped everything after Joe's death. Her night pharmacy courses, her softball, her friends. Boiled herself relentlessly down to just Mom-ness. And maybe, just maybe, she'd boiled away so much of her essence in the process that she'd stopped being Mom, too. Became just *a* mom. Which would never be enough for a ravenous, radiant little fireball like Natalie.

Who'd come back, now. Who was here to show Jess just how disappointed she was. "Benny, it's her. She's come for the kids. She's going to…" But even as she started to say that, the words died in her mouth. She knew it wasn't true. If it were Natalie—her Natalie—she wouldn't have rung the bell. Certainly not more than once. Not with her child in here.

Also, if it were Natalie, Jess would have known. And she would have let her in. Wouldn't have been able to help it.

*Homeless-kid supper?*

"Who is it?" she asked.

"Can I let him in?"

"Okay."

Benny's smile brightened. "Really?"

"Maybe. Move. I'll let him in."

Half-shoving Benny back toward the kitchen, Jess made for the door. If Benny saw her pick up the scissors on her way past the coffee table, he didn't say anything. She considered stopping at the front window, peering through the curtains. But what good would that have done? She snapped the deadbolt back and pulled open the door.

The scissors came up before Jess realized she'd lifted them, flicking open in her hand like a switchblade, and she had to scream inside her own head to keep her arm from jabbing forward and sticking the blades right into the kid.

Because that's who it was. Some pitiful, swaying, teenaged boy, pimpled, bleach-blond, his gauntness terrifying. That is, it made Jess terrified *for* him. From somewhere, he'd scavenged someone's cast-off straw hat, and he doffed it now. The straw had ripped around the perimeter, and when the kid lifted it, Jess could see evening sky through it. The first stars against the blackening gray.

"Hi," said the kid, started to put the hat back on, then kept it down at his chest. Like a little boy asking if his friend could come out to play. "Sorry. Is, uh, Benny home?"

"Come on in, Hon," Jess said. Only when the kid was past her, and past the bassinet, did she remember to lower the scissors.

Meedy, the kid said his name was, or Meaty. He took the plates Benny gave him and started setting the table, just like that. Wrongly, but neatly, the spoons upside down along the tops of the plates but aligned just so, the paper-towel napkins unfolded but tucked under the edges of the plates. He talked mostly to Benny, only occasionally glanced toward Jess, who'd settled on the couch. She'd fished out the kids, put them back on their play-mat with their plastic letter-blocks, but she'd eyed the teenager's every move, and almost jumped up to run him through when he stepped abruptly in her direction, trying what she realized only just in time was some goofy lip-twist for the benefit for the children.

This time, the kid noticed the scissors. He saw the look on Jess's face, too, and flinched, then blushed. From a pocket of his pathetic shirt, he fished out a harmonica. A toy harmonica. Red, with a train engine on top. It might as well have been a kazoo.

"Sorry," said Jess. "Old habit."

"Me, too," said the kid, and Jess wondered what he meant by that. He just stood there, now, looking uncertain. Then he glanced over his shoulder toward the kitchen, and Jess could actually see the hunger-spasms flit over his face.

Pitiful kid. Beautiful black roots of his hair just visible through his hideous, flaking bleach job, like good wood under layers of dust. When he looked back her way, she gestured at the harmonica.

"Well, go ahead. Let's hear."

The kid let loose, and both babies started shrieking. Amazingly, the kid didn't stop right away, seemed to think maybe the boys were singing along. Jess had to snap her fingers in his face to halt him.

He blinked, harmonica at his lips, tremulous half-grin just visible behind it.

"Don't try so hard," she said, as gently as she could, which wasn't that gently. This had become a challenging night. "Don't try to make us laugh."

"I wasn't."

"Just...play a song."

"I did. I was."

"Oh, yeah? What song was that?"

"'She'll Be Coming Round the Mountain?' You know, 'driving six white horses'..."

"Yeah, but she isn't screaming while she comes," Jess snapped, saw the poor kid flinch again, and all at once, she started to laugh. Just for this one moment. Gorgeous pancake smells flooding the air, children at her feet, a homeless boy deafening her with a harmonica. Somehow, a semblance of life had followed when she'd fled her life. Reconstituted itself around her.

The kid looked more baffled then ever. But he laughed, too.

Benny stuck his head out of the kitchen. "I can tell you one thing she'll be doing. She'll be eating these." With a flourish, he swept a platter full of pancakes into the room, and smells overwhelmed them.

For a long while, they sat and ate. To Jess, it all seemed almost too much, but completely irresistible, like sweet tea on a scalding summer day. At first, the kid shoveled whole pancakes into his mouth at a time. But as he slowed, he started to savor, and the look on his face—not unlike hers, she imagined, at once overwhelmed and lost and just a little sickened by something surprisingly close to bliss—cast a gentle glow over the table. There was nothing joyful about anything he told them—dealer father, junkie mother, he'd slept on the streets of DC in the spring but come here because the cops were kinder, the tourists more generous, and only the teens got violent—but he was still mostly a boy, in there, and he not only knew who Mark Belanger was but why the Orioles had kept playing someone who hit that badly, and his survival-slyness was evident at all times but not yet dominant. Benny kept catching her eye, and every time he did, she couldn't help but smile, which annoyed her, which just made him happier, which made her smile more. Outside, through the slit in the curtains she'd now drawn, she could see the white shine off the surface of the ocean, though not quite the ocean itself. Whatever this mood was, it had claimed even the babies, and they crawled over each other and their blocks and pulled themselves standing at the side of the couch and fell back on their butts and gurgled and laughed.

"I'll clean if you'll watch the babes," Jess told them, intending to let Benny bask in the glow he'd created.

But Benny said, "I'll help. Those babes are pretty close to sleeping."

And he joined her in the kitchen, and they kissed, washed dishes, kissed some more. She put a hand down the back of his jeans, squeezed, and he laughed and held her hand there. The last thing left on the table was the pitcher of still-hot, homemade syrup, and after a while Jess went to get that, and that's when she saw what was happening.

The kid, hunched over Benny's laptop. Typing.

Jess froze, syrup pitcher in one hand, just-dried skillet in the other. "What are you doing?" she said.

The kid jumped as if she'd poured the syrup over his head, half-turned toward her. Turned the laptop in the other direction. "Sorry. I should have asked. I just don't…you know, not much Internet access under the pier. It's…my favorite site. This musician. I was just…"

But Jess was behind him, now. Staring at the computer screen. Which wasn't *just*.

It was a Twitter page. Some guy whose face, in the profile photo, looked remarkably like this kid's. Only older. And nastier. Something about the mouth.

Underneath the profile photo was a photo of Jess. The one with Joe, in his black tango pants, from Myrtle Beach, three months before he died. Which she'd been sure Natalie had taken on the night she left.

*Hey, Tweetybirds*, the page read. *Seeking this woman. And her babies. Seen 'em? Whistle, and I'll come…*

She felt the impact of metal-on-skull through the handle of the pan. *Like vibrations down an aluminum bat*, she thought, terrified even as she followed all the way through, and the kid's head rocked back, banged off the edge of the desk, dragged the rest of him off the chair into a heap at her feet. For one moment, she let herself stand there, *made* herself look, see what she'd done.

*Bashed in the head of a helpless, homeless child. And very possibly killed him.*

Benny was behind her again. Not shouting. Again. His voice came out choked. "Jess? What on Earth—"

"Benny, it's time to run." She dropped the pan at her feet, and the syrup with it. Then she dropped to her knees, put her hand to the kid's bloodied temple, felt the beat there. Tears sprang to her eyes. She ignored them, held her hand to the kid's face for one moment more.

"Jess. Jesus Christ, you—"

Jerking to her feet, she collapsed the bassinet, started throwing blankets and toys toward the door. "Bag those up, Benny. Everything in the trunk. Come on."

"I'm not doing anything until you—"

"Benny, Benny, Benny, we have to *run*." And she was running, hurtling around the room.

She'd run, all right. But not away. Not anymore. Because Natalie's face was in front of her, again. Staring right down into Jess', and this time Jess let herself see. Let herself acknowledge what she'd been too angry or frustrated or just plain tired to acknowledge before. What she should have known all along. Natalie was Natalie. A little wild.

Way too hungry for the world, and so way too likely just to put it all in her mouth. But underneath the wildness—and all around it, and much stronger—was the daughter Jess had raised. Fierce and strong and loyal and loving and determined. And scared. That's what Jess hadn't been able to face, hadn't let herself see. Natalie had looked hard that night, yes. Had meant to terrify her mother. Had really meant to leave her son behind.

In order to save him.

In mid-sprint, as she snatched Benny's robe off the back of the door, she felt a sudden, stupid swell of pride. Because Natalie really was Natalie, after all.

The daughter she'd failed, in other words. Not by letting her make her mistakes, or become who she'd become. But by letting her go, and not standing by her.

Well, that was over, now.

"I'm coming," she murmured, hurling clothes and baby toys into her suitcase, Benny's suitcase. "Shit, Natalie, I'm coming."

She'd seen the woman standing by the back window the second she entered the bedroom—of course she had, how could she not have? — but somehow she didn't register her, or at least didn't stop. Was too busy. But when she lifted the suitcase and turned to the living room, she found the woman standing between her and the door. Stout, strong, pretty African American woman. Standing in her bedroom, where she could not possibly be. Smiling.

"You want to put that over on the bed, dear?" the woman said.

Then she leapt, catching Jess around the shoulders and twisting her face-first and down into the floor.

## It's Late

### *(24 hours earlier...)*

It took Natalie far too long, most of the rest of the night, to row the flatboat back up the narrow, root-choked tributary to the bait-shack pier where Sophie had stolen it and left the car. The whole time, Sophie just sat in the bow, wrapped in a mucky tarp she'd found in the bottom of the boat, shivering as a surprising small-hour chill seeped out of the black gums and hung in a gauzy, white haze on the surface of the water. Her wet hair obscured her eyes. She spoke only once, when they reached a fork in the waterway, and Natalie, who could barely restrain herself from leaping for the land and charging through the trees, hissed, "Well?"

Sophie didn't hesitate, nodded with her chin. "That way. Hurry up, why are you rowing so slow?"

Natalie could have brained her with the oar. Instead, she turned the boat and pulled. In truth, she was relieved that Sophie had immediately understood the situation. Had grabbed for Natalie's hand—causing one horrible moment of doubt, when Natalie thought her friend was going to pull her into the water to meet her scaly new pals—and scrambled back aboard.

But she also found it hard not to blame Sophie for taking them here in the first place, so far from where they needed to be, even if that was unfair. And more than once, she glanced up as she rowed to find Sophie gazing dreamily past her shoulder, back into the swamp. As though Natalie had plucked her out of summer camp.

Also, Natalie's whole face hurt where Sophie had bashed it against the GTO's dashboard. And the chill had slipped through her own swamp-sweat into her bones, so that only the rowing kept shivers from overwhelming her, too. Every single time she stopped moving, her Hunger stirred, seemed to unhinge, yawn wider, like an internal set of jaws that could swallow her whole.

As soon as they'd gotten in the car, Natalie floored the accelerator, pointing them straight north through tiny swamp-shack towns toward I-95. All too soon, sunlight started streaming through the forest to the east. Sophie kept glancing out the window, then over at Natalie, then back at the woods as they flushed with color. But she didn't say anything until the sun itself swept over the rim of the treetops and engulfed them.

"Natalie, *Jesus!*" Sophie flung her hands up, but didn't cover her eyes, not quite, and she didn't burst into flame or anything. Neither of them did. After her outburst, Sophie just scrunched in her seat, knees to her chest, hands thrown over her head, whimpering. But with her eyes open.

Which made complete sense to Natalie, even as she squirmed in her seat, bit almost through her bottom lip in an effort to stay still, not jerk the wheel and send them careening into the nearest shadows. They hadn't exploded. She'd known they wouldn't. The sun hurt, all right, probed at every nerve in her skin like a dental tool digging through root. She didn't think she could tolerate it for a whole day, maybe not even a whole hour. But she'd get as far as she could.

And in the meantime, through the agony and the haze of her own tears, she'd stare, like Sophie, at the way the world looked when it was lit. *How could she possibly have forgotten so quickly?* But she knew the answer to that. She hadn't forgotten, really. This sight—this impossible green, this radiant orange, the daily blossoming of the whole planet—couldn't be forgotten, because it couldn't be remembered. Could not be held in a human brain. That's what made it such a daily revelation. All her life, she'd been told that death was unimaginable, unknowable. When in truth, it was life that could never be imagined. Life was just too big.

She held out as long as she could—nowhere near long enough—and then skidded the car sideways down an embankment, across a dirt lot next to a baked, brown fallow field, and straight up against some sort of drain conduit, a giant cement cylinder. By the time she'd wrenched the key to off, Sophie had already fled for the shade, and Natalie stumbled from the driver's seat, barely even got the car door shut, and followed.

It wasn't exactly cool in the conduit, but after the swamp and the sun, the breeze in there felt sweet as a shower, and soothed them both. For a long while, they said nothing, stood with their arms out or lay flat like lizards with their limbs stretched across the skin of the cement, regulating their body heat as best they could manage. Occasional horse- or dragonflies buzzed at either end of the conduit, zipped through, twitched around their faces, zipped away again. Somewhere to their left, out in the tobacco fields just beyond this one, some sort of machine rumbled to life, close enough that they could feel its shudders in their feet and spines.

Eventually, Sophie straightened, backed halfway up the curve of one wall, and perched, still as a spider. Outside, the machine shuddered closer. Natalie stood, felt Eddie's ghost hands at her cheek. They couldn't wait for dark, she knew. Had to go. *Now.*

*Hold on*, she murmured inside her head, but to her son. *My sweet boy. Mama's coming.*

"You realize if someone finds us, we're going to have to do something. Right?" Sophie asked.

It wasn't just the words that made her cringe. It was the tone, so blank that even Natalie couldn't read it. But it made her hungry. No—reminded her how hungry she was. She stomped her foot like an eight-year-old, and ridiculous tears sprang to her eyes.

"Why, Sophie? Why do we have to?"

Sophie took a long time answering, and in the end said only, "Little feet. Little Roo feet," in the same unreadable voice.

The sun had reached its zenith, the colors out there going even richer as midday shadows swirled into and suffused them, when Natalie pulled Sophie off the wall and led her toward the opening of the conduit. Sophie started to protest, glanced at Natalie's face, and stopped. They were standing right at the conduit's mouth, pushing pointless air in and out as though preparing for a deep-sea dive, when the girls appeared.

Three of them, maybe ten or eleven years old, in flip-flops and baggy shorts. Two wore floral bikini tops, and one a baggy Four Corners Pizza Pie T-shirt. *Because of what was happening to her body*, Natalie knew instantly, remembering that age with a clarity that stunned her. Remembering being that age with Sophie. Remembering watching Sophie's sudden, startling curves with the most disquieting mixture of dread and envy. The girl before her now wore braided blond pigtails, and had an unlit cigarette in her mouth. Skin beaded with perfect pearls of sweat.

*So tasty…*

She was literally in mid-lunge, half off her feet and flying, when Sophie caught her around the wrist and ripped her backward, almost tore her shoulder out of its socket. Turning, snarling in surprise, Natalie stared into Sophie's face. Which was blank. Not friendly, not sad, nothing.

The girls, squealing, had already scurried away. Natalie could hear their sandals flapping in the dirt like grasshopper wings.

"Why?" Natalie growled.

Sophie didn't answer.

"I thought you wanted me to."

"I do."

"I thought you couldn't fucking wait for me to Finish."

"I can't."

Natalie stared, felt those jaws inside her close just slightly, slip just barely back into the cave they'd hollowed out for themselves. Moray eel in her esophagus.

Sophie stared back. Didn't look angry. Didn't look sad. "You can't eat them," she said. "Not those girls."

And Natalie grabbed her. Hugged her. Sophie did not hug her back. "Come on," Natalie said. "We're going. We have to go."

"This is going to hurt," said Sophie.

And it did, the second the light touched them. The pain proved even worse than it had a few hours earlier, but once they'd reached the car, Sophie threw herself in the back under the tarp from the boat, and Natalie kept the pedal down, and leaned away from the windows as far as she could. Only her knees remained directly in the light, and they burned like someone was pressing an iron down on them but didn't smoke, didn't turn red, just scalded. Eventually, some unimaginable stretch of time from now, it would be evening. She pushed the pedal even harder, and they flew.

As the royal blue overhead finally began to darken, and the moon rose, and Venus with it, Sophie rummaged under her seat, came up with a cassette, and jammed it in the deck without looking at it. Buddy Holly. Raving on. For a few seconds, he sounded so sweet in Natalie's ears, a warm, wild wind she could sail forever. Then he didn't, and she punched off the radio.

"Why?" Sophie asked.

Natalie didn't answer.

"Come on, Nat. I need the distraction."

"I don't," Natalie said, edging forward in her seat, as though that could coax just a little more speed from the GTO.

Four times, they got pulled over, had to waste precious seconds staring into cops' eyes and leaving them quivering in their wake. Each time, Sophie had to clamp Natalie in her seat, murmur low and steady to keep her from leaping out of the car, tearing at the soft, sweat-dewed throat-meat hovering just out her window like a drooping flower, so close she could smell not just the skin but the sweet life beneath it. The last cop was a woman, fifty or so, silver-black hair just starting to thin. It rolled in the wind like the crown of a tree, and Natalie waited for Sophie's iron-firm clamp around her wrist, then looked up in alarm as Sophie's door slammed.

Buzzing, paralyzed, she watched Sophie make her way around the car, waltz right up to the woman, who barked at her to stop, started to pull her gun, and went still. Sophie's hands flashed out, but only to cup the woman behind the neck, pull her close. The kiss Sophie gave her took forever, looked so soft, like biting into a nectarine. Except not biting. Again, as Sophie pulled away, Natalie found herself watching through a film of tears.

"Why did you do that?" she whispered when Sophie climbed back in beside her, though she was already revving the engine, peeling them back out into the traffic.

"She just looked so small," Sophie said, in a manner that somehow communicated profound understanding and no compassion whatsoever. "She's trying so hard. It's hard being her."

In the rearview mirror, Natalie could see the cop standing in front of her bike. Hand to her mouth and the wind in her hair.

They arrived at Honeycomb Corner just after two A.M. Natalie knew her child wouldn't be there—she would, in fact, have killed her mother if he had been, provided the Whistler hadn't already taken care of that—but she still experienced a spasm of nostalgia as she gunned the GTO up Sardis, past the rows of perfectly ordered and trimmed pines, neat and unreal as hedges in a child's drawing, past the square, leafy subdivisions they'd never been able to afford to move to, the park with its moon-white teeter-totter and baby swings that the city kept not only oiled but painted. *I was an alien amongst you even then*, Natalie thought, watching the houses, the lights already off in almost all of them. *Though I never meant to be.*

And then she realized that what she felt had little to do with nostalgia. Was, in fact, even more inane, under the circumstances. This was simply the place where she'd lived with her mom. The place where she'd gone whole hours—just occasionally, every now and then—believing she was safe. Believing that enough to forget, sometimes, that there was any other way to be. When she saw Caution tape stretched across the entrance to the trailer park, she stomped the brakes so hard that the GTO squealed and bucked before skidding to a stop.

"*Shit,*" Natalie hissed.

"Shit," Sophie agreed. Blankly.

"Oh, no," said Natalie. Then she was out of the car, leaving it in the middle of the road, darting into the less-trimmed trees that ringed the rows of trailers. Behind her, she heard Sophie moving the car to the shoulder, which was probably smart, but her attention remained riveted on the rows of silent, pathetic temp-homes parked in their berths. *Like house-souls that missed the boat from heaven,* Wanda had announced, once, through her eighth or ninth gin and tonic of a long-ago spring evening. Houses that were meant to be homes, but lost their way somehow, got shunted here. And became something else. Color-form-homes. Homes pasted in easily removable places by little-kid angels. Practice homes.

Home enough for her, though. And for her son. Almost.

She could see her trailer, now. Door hanging open, so that the night washed in and out of it. Windows open, but no audible baseball chatter. Not her home anymore, or her mom's, either. No one's home.

And anyway, the Caution tape wasn't around that trailer. It was around Wanda's.

Sophie joined her in her crouch near a stubby pine completely consumed by kudzu. "What the fuck?" she said.

For answer, Natalie stepped out of the shadows into the trailer park. She expected cops to appear from everywhere. Or the Whistler to drop on her like a bobcat. Nothing happened. No one moved, anywhere. In that new family's trailer, the Walshes', just down the row, she heard the usual thudding garbage-rock, but turned low. So low that the walls of their double-wide didn't even bulge. A new knife-edge of fear trailed down Natalie's back, launched her straight across the dirt towards her mother's trailer. She took the front steps in one jump, stuck her head in the door.

A pot she recognized on the stove. A stupid, saggy white blouse of her mom's, with an old coffee stain on the front, discarded across the bed. The sweet feelings she'd had back in the GTO were gone, now. There was nothing here. Or rather, the only thing left on this earth worth finding wasn't here. Thank God.

She whirled, left the trailer, moved to Wanda's with Sophie in tow. She could smell the dried blood from fifteen feet away, had just spotted the brown, crusted splotch of it that had seeped under Wanda's door from inside, when the older Walsh boy stepped out of his own weed-cloud into the moonlight. Natalie grabbed him by the frayed collar of his Megadeth shirt and banged him to the dirt so hard that half of what he'd just smoked burst from his lungs like dust off a beaten rug. Then she straddled his chest.

"Natalie?" he coughed. "Right? You're Natalie?"

"What happened?"

"*Natalie?*" His red, dumb eyes widened in their bony sockets while his greasy hair soaked up the dirt and his surprisingly gentle mouth curved into a smile somehow younger *and* wiser than his sixteen or whatever years. Natalie remembered noticing that mouth once, not too long ago, when the family first moved in. *Christ, probably less than two months ago. Earlier this summer.* That mouth, she had thought, would get this kid more of what he wanted than he expected to get. Would get him in trouble, not all of it bad.

Assuming he lived that long. And stopped looking at her the way he was looking at her now.

"You look—" the kid started, and Natalie lifted him by the collar and slammed him down again. His jaws jumped in their sockets, and his eyes rolled back.

"What. Happened?"

Whether from the weed, the Natalie-effect, or the pounding she'd given his head, the Walsh kid seemed unable to respond. Kept trying to wet that pretty mouth with his little-boy tongue.

"Did my mom say anything?" Natalie growled, knowing it was hopeless. Knowing Jess wouldn't have. Certainly not to this kid.

"Your mom's gone? Where'd she go?"

To keep from screaming—and also from ripping her teeth straight through this kid's throat—Natalie bent forward fast, kissed him on the forehead, and stood up.

"Whoa, Tiger," she heard Sophie call, in that infuriating, inflection-less tone, as she half-ran down the row of trailers toward the trees. By the time she reached them, she'd started to wretch, and her muscles clenched, partly from panic, partly from the desperate need to turn around, go back. Get someone. And eat him.

Sophie didn't say anything once she reached Natalie's side, just put her hand on her friend's bent back. The touch so cold, like an ice-pack, without the therapeutic properties.

"Get off," Natalie said when she could.

"Sweetie," said Sophie, "you should eat something. You'll feel better."

That annoyed Natalie enough to drag her upright. She stared into Sophie's eyes. "Is that supposed to be cute? Funny?"

"What would be funny about it?"

They got back in the car, started the engine, and Natalie realized she had no idea where to go or what to try. She watched her arms jiggling with the vibrations, which came simultaneously from the car and inside her. Along with everything else—rage, frustration, heartbreak—she realized that most of what she felt was relief.

*He's gone,* she thought. *He's safe. Not mine, not ever. But safe.*

"Oh, Mom," she murmured. "Thank you." A smell filtered into her nostrils. Blood smell. From the Walsh kid. From Wanda's trailer. Whether this was memory of smell or super-heightened sensory overload she had no idea. But she realized, finally, what the Wanda smell had to mean. What it suggested had happened here. And she found herself murmuring again. "I'm so sorry, Wanda. I'm so sorry." Then she jammed the car into gear and drove.

They went nowhere, rode the bicycle-spoking wide streets in and out of empty, useless downtown Charlotte, back and forth, and wound up parked just off Providence, at the edge of the glowing, green expanse of Queens University. All that perfect grass and scrubbed, red brick. All those trees, fat with leaves. The whole campus a near-perfect replica of the Ivies it so desperately emulated, and yet so Charlotte. Personality-less. Blank. When Natalie abruptly left the car and wandered into the quad, she saw no one. Felt no wind. Felt like she was walking on the stage set of a college quad, even though the place really was a hundred fifty years old. *I come,* she thought, *from a giant suburb with no urb. A city with quadrants named for its malls. A sprawling, beautifully maintained hollow. A vampire city, constantly devouring itself, and so staying new. Which turns out to be such a different thing than staying alive.*

Glancing over her shoulder, she saw Sophie standing by the car, half-watching. Looking bored. If anyone had come by just then, what would Sophie have done? Fucked them? Staggered them with a lust so pure it would poison love forever? Eaten them, out of gluttony? Killed them, for sport? Given them just enough of a glimpse of what they could have had, what could have come for them, that they'd stay haunted and lonely and grateful for the rest of their lives?

Was that what she would do, when Eddie was safe? When she'd eaten? When there were just years of nights ahead, and nothing with which to fill them?

She did scream, then. Long. Loud.

No one came. No lights in any windows. Even Sophie barely looked up. As though Natalie hadn't screamed at all. Wasn't even there.

And then, at last, she knew where to go. What to try next. On unsteady legs, she returned to the car.

"Where are we headed?" said Sophie, but not as though she cared.

"To see Benny. And Hewitt."

For the first time all night, Sophie seemed surprised. "Hewitt?"

"If my mom told anybody, she'd have told one of them."

"Hewitt," Sophie said. Natalie still couldn't read her voice. But it had lost its blankness. And Natalie had a realization, one she should have come to long ago. Of course, Hewitt had been Sophie's camp counselor, too. Of course, they'd stayed up late at sleepovers for years afterward, concocting Hewitt-fantasies in the dark. And of course, Natalie knew, Sophie loved her so desperately—really had imagined that their lives would never take them more than a street or two apart, ever, long before the night the Whistler found them—that she'd have done almost anything to ensure that.

Or maybe anything.

"Jesus Christ," she said as she wound the GTO through the brightly lit, empty neighborhoods back toward Sardis Road. "You crazy, fucked-up bitch."

"Excuse you?"

"I can't believe…no, I *can*, that's the incredible part."

"Oh, Honey. We really need to get some food in you."

"You must have done it, what, days after I did? You didn't just have to go get pregnant, too, you had to—"

Sophie made a siren sound. Kept making it. "You, the brooding hottie in the GTO. Pull over. Reckless thinking."

"Hewitt is Roo's father, too, isn't he?"

Sophie stopped making the siren sound. Turned full in her seat, and stared at Natalie. After a long moment, she said, "What? *Ewww…*" She started laughing. "Why would I do that? Especially after your description of the festivities." Her laugh became a full-blown giggle fit. And Natalie—despite the Hunger, the panic, everything—found herself laughing with her. Just for one moment.

Then they were in the Waffle House parking lot, under the stupid yellow sign, and there he was through the window. The father of her child. Tall and clean and bushy-headed, leaning over to refill the syrup canister on someone's table. Permanent, clueless half-smile right where it always was.

"Natalie," Sophie said. Still blank, but low. "I want my Roo."

Hewitt saw them the second they walked in the door. "Where have you guys *been*?" he shouted all the way across the restaurant, swinging every eye in the place toward them. That was fine with Natalie. It would shut them all up quicker. She walked straight between the booths, ignoring the stares from all sides. Something in her shoulders released, just a little, as she realized what she'd very much feared she'd find here, too. *Believed* she would find: more Caution tape. More blood, already drying. Dried.

*But he hadn't come here.*

*Because he'd somehow found out what he needed to know at Honeycomb Corner? Or because coming here hadn't occurred to him?*

"Where's Benny?" she snarled, and to her own surprise stepped into the hug Hewitt had instinctively opened his arms to offer. At her touch, he quivered. But not that much. *Because he was the father of her child, and somehow resistant?*

No. Because he was Hewitt. And almost miraculously oblivious to everyone else.

Except here he was *pushing her back*, even. Holding her at arms' length. Though having to glance down at his knees, which had gone to jelly on him, in order to do so.

"Hey, Nat, I'm so glad you're here. I've been meaning to talk to you. I've been kind of freaky needing to."

There was something new under his half-smile. Or maybe it had always been there. Whatever it was, it wasn't anything the sight of new-

Natalie had drawn from him. She waited, wondering.

"I want to see Eddie," he said. "I want to see my son."

Natalie's mouth opened—either to answer that with the scorn it deserved, or just to eat him and get it over with—and then the muscles in her face went slack. As though this pathetic guy had somehow sucked out some of the poison. Not enough, but a little. Out of nowhere, she missed her father. Air-guitaring and duckwalking through his pineapple upside-down days. Throwing his daughter in the air. Kissing his wife repeatedly on the mouth, though she'd already frozen up too much with grief to kiss him back. Just like her mother, Natalie had known he was going. Had been unable to keep him proper company, or even comfort him, much. But he'd gone out singing.

"Me, too," Natalie whispered.

"What? What are you talking about? Where have you been? You just disappear, and I know I've been a jackass and kinda lost, but I want to see him. I want to be part of—"

Sophie flipped him so hard off his feet onto the nearest table top that Natalie thought she'd broken his back. The multiple *crack* noises could have been wood, ribs, or both. The Egyptian-looking guy who'd been sitting at the table just sat with his mouth agape, syrup oozing down his unknotted purple tie, eyes misty with lust.

"Where are they?" Sophie hissed in Hewitt's face.

Still strangely dazed, Natalie shook her own head, touched Sophie's arm. "She means Benny."

Sophie lifted Hewitt by the shoulders and banged him down again. "Where's Benny?" Then she glanced back at Natalie. "We're asking about Benny?"

"What *are* you talking about?" Hewitt was babbling. Panicking.

Natalie nudged Sophie aside, leaned over. He stared back up, wide-eyed. And not in love with her. Which almost made her love him. This guy she'd had a fling and a child with. It made the same stupid sense as everything else about living.

"Hewitt. Right now. I need to talk to Benny."

"Well, talk to him."

"He's here?"

If possible, Hewitt's eyes went even more bewildered. "What do you mean? He went off with your mom."

Natalie had to grab the plastic booth cover and the Egyptian guy's head to keep from falling. Get herself steady. She glanced at Sophie. Thinking, *good for you, Mom.*

And then, *You stupid idiot.* Because Jess really could have dropped off the planet if she'd thought she had to. Would have *left* the planet, if she'd believed that was the only way to protect her child. Children.

But Benny. Who loved so many people. Loved people, period...

Her legs steady again, her spine a seam of diamond down her back, Natalie leaned over Hewitt and stared upside-down right into his eyes. "Hewitt. I know you know. I know he calls here. Where is he?"

## Wild Women
## Don't Worry

*Even now, after countless repetitions, the moment brought Mother a sensation so acute it verged on delight. Stepping into the bedroom doorway, she'd come face to face with the frayed cotton ball of a guy with the dishrag on his arm, registered the astonishment on his face, and without even bothering to catch his eye, said, "Bring me a towel, Sugar? Bit of a mess in here."*

*And without so much as blinking, let alone asking who she was or how she'd gotten into his condo, the guy had spun on his heel and gone and done it. Not because Mother had turned on the charm either (which she couldn't exactly help, but rarely bothered accentuating), but because he was a well-meaning— and therefore congenitally guilty—white guy, with a black woman asking.*

*It had caught her completely by surprise, the first thousand times it had happened. Way back before the Whistler, even, when she was still close enough to before to remember what before felt like. She'd claimed the Whistler at least in part because of this very feeling. Along with the simple, impossible fact that she could. That a boy—a* white *boy—from a family of people who wouldn't have touched her with their spit, would fall so deeply under her spell that he'd beg her to take him, to make him like her, had charged their whole first decade together. Had probably provided the charge that allowed her to change him in the first place.*

*Cotton-ball guy got almost all the way back across the living room before the penny dropped. Even then, he didn't stop, just slowed, and his smiled twitched but didn't slip. He was still offering the towel on an outstretched arm, so Mother grabbed him around his wrist and broke it. Then she punched him full in the face, caught him as he collapsed, and tossed him on top of the little mama face-down on the rug behind her.*

*Except that the little mama wasn't face-down anymore. She'd rolled herself onto what had to be at least a few cracked ribs, and was just looking at Mother through shattered glasses.*

Losing my touch, *Mother thought, then thought of the Whistler and cursed aloud.*

*"Oh my God," said a voice over her shoulder, and Mother swiveled, coiling. What she saw confused her still more, and caused her to grunt in frustration. Who were all these idiots?*

*Holding a hand to his head, staggering up from under the desk as though he'd just emerged through a trap door, came a reedy, ridiculous kid. Moles all over his muscle-less forearms and a cheap, straw hat tumbling off his lap. "You're* her."

*It had been so long since Mother had shivered that for a moment, she literally couldn't imagine what was happening.* She could still shiver? *Apparently, she could, if she got bewildered or alarmed or angry enough.*

*Or—*seriously?*—*lonely *enough? Because that was definitely happening, now. And she knew why. This kid reminded her far too much of her man. Her man at the beginning, all white and thin and awestruck and new.*

*"Who do you think I am?" she murmured, her voice positively horse.*

*"Her! His manager. But how did you get here so quick? I just posted, what, twenty minutes ago?" His questions came faster as his thoughts apparently started to clear, though he kept wincing and pressing a fist to the purple bruise on his temple. Mother wasn't really listening, but she caught enough of what he was saying—and had also noted, finally, the image on the computer monitor on the desk—to sort, at last, what must have happened. The realization made her laugh outright.*

*"That stupid website? It actually worked for something? You posted to tell him where they are, didn't you?"*

*The kid went right on babbling, so Mother caught his eye and shut him up. His mouth sagged open, and his eyes rolled back, then locked in on her. Boy-crush on the Whistler forgotten, just like that. To her amazement, Mother almost felt guilty.*

*"He's not for you, Hon," she said. "I'm saving you a world of grief."*

*The kid's eyes welled with tears, and Mother grunted again. Somehow, the Whistler had imprisoned her inside one of his horrible songs, a full-on Nashville weepie. Broken hearts and bad intentions all around. So be it.*

*She stepped toward the kid, and then, for one moment, halted. If she hadn't known better—if the near-century adrift in the currentless, depthless dark hadn't forced her to acknowledge the truth—she might have mistaken this feeling for heartache. Or regret. One of those useless, half-invented, paralyzing emotions humans spent their entire adult lives pretending they hated feeling. In their songs—crammed with witty, worthless words, infused with melody those words didn't deserve and couldn't sustain—they called it everything but what it really was: rote nostalgia, nothing more, for something they'd lost the moment they were born. That tangible connection to anything else that lived.*

*Not that calling the sensation by its name helped much. Because oh, it was powerful, even to Mother. She caught herself now just looking at this kid. Pale, paltry boy, so lost and thin and in love with the music he must have just learned how to hear. He would worship her, if she let him. Already did, in fact. Would stare at her for years to come out of eyes still haunted by the world as he saw it right now. The one he still believed had something better in it than what he'd known so far, if he could only find it.*

*She still found it just a little intoxicating, honestly. That ghostly trace of hope…*

Was its pull still strong enough that she could take him with her? Transform this kid, and move on? Leave the Whistler to his Destiny, for all the happiness he'd find there? Was it her own emotion, or the kid's, that needed to be strong enough to make whatever happened happen?

*As had occurred more than once in Mother's long, long existence, it was that split-second of hesitation that placed her in danger. And the ferocity of* resolve that always followed that saved her. Because at the exact moment the little mama drove the scissors into her neck, she was already lunging forward to kill the boy. And so, though both blades bit deep, driving into her spinal cord and then ripping upward, they just missed severing things as her own teeth locked around the kid's carotid and ground together. The pain was stunning, even frightening, she'd felt nothing like it for so impossibly long, and she roared through clenched jaws and jerked sideways and actually beheaded the kid without intending to. Straightening, she watched his head bounce once on the carpet and land sideways, facing her, the eyes astonished, still aware, and—wow, that could really happen?—blinking. Welling up. Understanding.

Well. Mother always did love providing clarity.

She turned her back on the spurting, expiring kid and slammed Jess over the dining room table into the wall. Reaching over her shoulder, she caught the curved top of the scissor-handle—barely, because the little mama had driven it almost all the way down into the skin, had good and meant it, Mother had to give her that—started to pull, half-screamed with the thrill of the agony, and then stopped. Stared down at Jess where she lay in a heap against the baseboards.

She'd leave the scissors right where they were. Let the little mama see.

The little mama saw. Oh, yes, she did. Although she came closer to hiding it than any living thing Mother had interacted with in a very long time. Fascinated, she watched the mama watch her.

Then the mama stirred. Let herself wince, just once. And said, "You're what happened to my daughter."

*Mother burst into a grin. If she'd known it could be like this, she would have broken up with the Whistler decades ago. "I'm much worse," she said, kneeling down, feeling the delicious, warm wet spreading through the carpet around her, and staring the little mama squarely in the face. "I'm what happened to what happened to your daughter. Now, let's see, here…"*

*Standing, still a little wobbly, the scissors making an actual* clink *somewhere in the back of her chest like her own personal bell clapper, Mother finally got the moment she needed to assess the room. She didn't love what she saw. To get at the Whistler in this space, she'd have to let him in. And once he was in, with so little room for surprise or maneuvering, they'd just be fighting. Mother was far too much the realist to like her chances that way. Her eyes alighted briefly on the reedy boy's head, which was no longer blinking, just wide-eyed. Little spurty pumpkin head. For a second, she thought that the pathetic croak she'd just heard came from there. Then, finally, she saw the bassinet.*

*"No," moaned the little mama, before she could stop herself, and Mother felt that grin flicker on her face again. Like heat, almost. Like actual happiness. She went straight to the bassinet, bent over it, found one baby sleeping, the other rubbing his eyes. They'd missed all the fun. She'd see to it they didn't miss any more.*

*"This is going to take a while," she said. "Need to get ready."*

*Turning to make sure the little mama understood what was about to happen, Mother was astonished to find the woman halfway to her already, dragging herself sideways along the carpet. Which had to* hurt, *in her condition.*

*Whatever her injuries actually were, they were severe enough to slow her. Make anything she thought she might try utterly futile. And yet here she came.*

*"You know, I could get to like you," Mother said, and drove the spiked heel of her boot straight down into the back of Jess's hand.* Wow, is that floorboard I'm feeling, *Mother thought?* Did that really go all the way through?

*The little mama cried out. Stopped slithering. But her head didn't drop. And her eyes, behind their shattered lenses and a cloudburst of tears, left Mother's face only once, to shoot a glance at the window. As though she'd suddenly come up with the idea of escaping, instead of attacking. But Mother suspected this woman would not be thinking that. If only because she'd know better. She was a realist, too, this one. Like Mother. Except for the believing-she-could-do-anything-about-this part. They stared at each other, now. Mother and mother. The little mama's eyes riveted. No more window glances.*

*"What do you want?" the wounded woman asked.*

*Mother was so delighted that this resilient little creature could even speak, and so gratified by the clarity of the question, that she actually lifted her heel momentarily. Not that that probably eased the mama's pain any, since the movement still left half a boot-heel embedded in the hole in her hand.*

*"Right," she said. "That's so right. That's the heart of everything, isn't it? What do I want? Have I mentioned I'm just impressed as peaches with you?"*

*As a cautionary measure—and because she really was impressed—Mother drove the heel back down, spiking Jess to the floor. "Here's the thing, little mama. I've been thinking about that a lot. For days, really. See, I know what he wants. My man. My…ex, is that what today's woman calls them? He wants*

**215**

*your daughter. And see, I've barely even met your daughter, but I'm pretty perceptive, as a rule, and I understand exactly what she wants, too. She's just a whole mess of wants, actually. None of which she's going to get, I'm afraid.*

*"But me?" On sudden intuition, Mother glanced over her own shoulder at the window. And saw a window, with mostly drawn curtains. Blackness outside. Faint hiss of ocean susurration seeping through. With a shrug, she returned her attention to Jess. "At first, I think I thought I wanted him back, if you can believe that. I guess I'm pretty much an old-fashioned gal, at heart. But then, of course, I started wondering why. For what? I mean, he's right, what he says, never mind the vain, stupid way he says it: I probably never exactly loved him—whatever that means—in the first place. Any more than he did me. So nope, I don't want that, either."*

*Under her heel, the woman stirred, and Mother bore down still harder, saying, "Hold on, hold on, now, you did ask. My next thought, and I just bet you'll understand this, was that I wanted to make him pay. As a matter of fact, until about sixty seconds ago, I still thought that."*

*With a sigh, Mother dropped her gaze to the little mama's. Peered right into those icy blues behind their shattered lenses. "But you know what? As it turns out? I just want to be the last one standing."*

*Yanking and then shaking her heel free of Jess's ruined hand, she turned and moved through the inch-deep puddle of the kid's still-spouting blood back to the bassinet. Bending, she scooped up the first squirming babe, then glanced fast back at Jess, half-expecting her to have writhed forward once more. Apparently, though, the woman had finally broken. She just lay there, staring at the window, as though she couldn't bear to watch. Well, Mother liked when they watched. So she waved the kid in the air.*

*"I'll need this," she said, bent again and grabbed the other kid. "This, too. Ah, that's better."*

*And it was. Jess wasn't just watching, she'd even whimpered again. Just once, before controlling herself. But so sweetly and pitifully. Holding both kids under one arm, stacked like bread-loaves, squeezing just enough to keep them from squirming, Mother went to the kitchen and collected an apron with side pockets into which she could tuck the carving knives. "Need these," she said, and rattled the knives together as she strolled past Jess into the bedroom, where she caught sight of the cotton-ball guy, about whom she'd all but forgotten. He'd yet to stir, was just lying where Mother had dumped him. Or, actually— and Mother liked this even better—where the little mama had shoved him as she'd struggled out from underneath.*

*Gazing down, she thought a moment, then shook her head. "Can't think of any reason I need that, though." She lifted her boot to drive it through the guy's skull.*

*Yet again, the little mama cried out. Mama paused with her boot in the air and glanced that way.*

*The woman had her lips clamped shut, as though she regretted reacting. Was biting any additional reaction back.*

*"You might as well let it out, Dear," Mother said. "What are you saving it for?" Then, unsure exactly why, she lowered her boot next to the cotton-ball guy's head. Rested her toe against it, and thought awhile. Abruptly, she moved*

*back to Jess, knelt before her. She clanked all over the place, the knives in the apron and the scissors against her spine. Strangely satisfying.*

*"Tell you what, little mama," she said. "In just a little while, we're going to put my little plan into action. And I'm going to offer you a deal, of sorts."*

*Jess's expression didn't alter, and her eyes never wavered.*

*"Here it is. See, I don't actually care if you die. You understand? I don't even care if the children die, though realistically, the chances of both of them, or maybe either of them…the point is, you're all just means to an end. So if you stop trying to stick things in me, and you do exactly what I say, exactly when I say it, maybe we can…"*

*Her voice trailed off, and she stared just a little longer into Jess's face. And the feeling that filled her at that moment felt more like an actual emotion than any she'd experienced in so impossibly long. Years and years and years. She didn't have a name for it. But she was pretty sure it had something to do with sorrow.*

*"You're right," she said. "Never mind." Standing, she hauled the little mama to her feet by the scruff of her neck and settled both babies against the knives on her hip. "Let's take a walk."*

## Under the Boardwalk

## 1

*Leaving Natalie shuddering and whimpering in the front seat, Sophie threw off the reeking tarp under which she'd huddled for yet another eleven hours and staggered out of the car into the evening. Which was finally dark enough. Dark enough. Plenty dark enough. Standing in the middle of the empty street, in this dump of a town that reminded her mostly of the not-Myrtle Beach shitholes her mother had been able to afford for their two-day summer seaside escapes, she threw her arms wide and closed her eyes and let the coolness funnel over and around her. Salt spray and seawind and moonlight. Best shower ever.* Partly because it came at the end of this dismal day—a second straight day, for god's sake, as in not night, under the tarp in the back, baking, listening to Natalie whine while her skin sizzled and the car jerked all over the road but somehow just kept going, because Natalie just had to go now, right now, even if it killed her, even if she wound up useless when they arrived, which was pretty much what had happened—*and partly because Natalie was still blubbering away back in the car. Out of earshot. Which left Sophie alone in the air.*

*Of course, Sophie had to give it up to her friend, on one level. She'd actually done it. Driven the sun down. All those merciless hours. But that didn't mean Sophie wanted to be locked in the same space with her even one second longer.*

*And besides. She wanted to see her Roo. Who, if Hewitt was right—he'd blurted out where Benny called from before Natalie had even gotten the Waffle House phone off its cradle—was in that corner condo over there, not fifteen yards away.*

*Her Roo. Waiting for her. She half-imagined she could hear him already. His hungry little seagull cry. His little feet. She took two long strides toward the condo, just past the streetlight poking its weak, yellow beam through the fog, and stopped.*

Why had she stopped?

*Instinct, that's why.*

*Natalie wouldn't have cared. Would have ignored every alarm bell shrieking in her brain and stormed in there. Would, in fact, be doing that momentarily, the second her skin cooled enough to let her. Which would be so stupid. So very Natalie. So why, Sophie wondered, did the thought trouble her so much?*

Because I'm not doing it. Because I am apparently capable of resisting it. Because…

*With a grunt, she hunched into her coat and hurried off the sidewalk into the bushes so she could creep to the condo's lone front window. Whoever was in there had drawn the curtains almost completely. But not quite. She could see a sliver of yellow. Even right beside it, crouching low, she couldn't hear anything over the drumming of ocean against sand across the street. But if she stood, stuck an eye in that sliver, she might just see.*

*She stood. Saw blood, so much blood, spattered all over the walls, completely coating the shade on the table lamp, dripping off its edges like fringe from a shawl. A body on the floor, still pumping sludge out its headless top like an uncapped oil well. Natalie's mom lay curled crazily against the wall near the dining room table, while the dark woman stood over her, and suddenly turned this way…*

Had she ducked fast enough? *For a long moment, Sophie crouched, ready, at the opening of the door, to flee the darkness, just flat run. But the door didn't open. The curtains didn't even move. She hadn't been seen. Not by that woman. The Whistler's companion, or mother, or pimp, or whatever she was. Sophie's instincts had been dead right; they were already here. Although she hadn't seen the Whistler himself yet.*

Which meant he was right behind her.

*She whirled, scraping her shoulder against the splintery white wall, and found nothing. Fog, floating spray. The GTO, with Natalie's shape still huddled in it.*

So, not behind her, then. But near. In there, probably.

Had Jess seen her? *Sophie's glimpse had been momentary, and the blood and that woman's presence had distracted her. But somehow, Sophie suspected Jess had indeed. The suspicion came less from anything she'd observed than from knowing Jess. But Sophie felt pretty certain, anyway. She edged her eyes up over the sill once more, peered through. Caught Jess looking right at her, and ducked again.*

*So. Yes. For whatever good that could possibly do.*

*Then she processed the rest of what she'd seen, the second time. That woman no longer over Jess, but standing by the bassinet. Holding her Roo.*

*Lunging to her feet, Sophie started inside, glanced back, saw the GTO's door open. On instinct—yet again—she reversed course and moved back down the sidewalk toward the car, keeping to the shadows. When she heard the condo door open, she almost threw herself prostrate in the stairwell of the nearest building, hoping it would hide her, then just kept going, fast, not even letting herself turn her head.*

*She found Natalie on her knees, shielded by the shadows and her open door from the sight of whomever might have emerged from the condo. She was still weeping, though she'd stopped whining, and had her arms out to catch the cooling air on her skin, which somehow looked even more pale than usual and also blazing red all at once. Why the sight of her like that—helpless, at least for a few seconds longer, not yet aware of what was happening down the block— caused Sophie such relief, she couldn't have said.*

*"You look like a poached egg," she said. "With ketchup."*

*Only then did she let herself glance back, just in time to see the procession.*

*That woman, with a body slung over her shoulder, and some bundles under one arm. Jess stumbling before her, almost doubled over, arms tight to her ribs, head down. As Sophie watched, they crossed the street and vanished down the wooden steps that led under the pier to the beach.*

*Turning back, she found Natalie staring at her. Halfway up off her knees, eyes clearing.* "Well?"

*For just a moment, Sophie considered. But there was nothing for it. Nothing else to do or say but the facts.* And how could there be, under the circumstances? *Eventually, she shrugged.* "She has him," *she said, watched Natalie tilt sideways, grab the door, bite back a shriek.* "She has them both."

*Just like that, Natalie got hold of herself. Went still.* "Has who? Who has them?" *She pulled herself to her feet.*

*This time, Sophie almost felt like applauding. Or just laughing at her. Nat Queen Cold. Risen from the dead. Again.* "That woman. The Whistler's woman. She has my Roo. And Eddie. She already killed somebody, maybe a couple somebodies, 'cause there is a lot of mess, and now she's got the kids and your mom over there down by the…"

So predictable, *Sophie thought, watching Natalie's back as it hurtled away from her, straight for the beach.* And so obviously the wrong move. Tactically ridiculous.

*But there was that voice again, nagging deep down in her brain where she couldn't quite reach to strangle or bury it. Pointing out that she was still just standing here.*

*Shrugging once more, Sophie crept off into the shadows. Maybe she could use the Natalie-stupidity to her advantage. Edging up against the seawall, she peered over and saw her best friend sailing silently down the steps, flying toward the group. Which hadn't seen her. Not yet.*

*Then, instead of continuing down to help, she turned to the pier and slipped out along it, directly over their heads.*

## 2

In *The Oresteia*, Natalie remembered from 9th-grade English, the avenging demons were called Furies. And once they came for you, they kept coming. Could not be shaken. Ever. And what infuriated them or brought them down upon you was matricide. *Which,* she thought as she flew, her feet barely seeming to stir the sand and making less sound than the floating moisture in the air, *makes them roughly half as Furious as I am.*

Even in full sprint, Natalie realized the woman should have heard her coming. *That* woman should have. But she had already launched herself, was plunging through the air with her hands out and her fingers curled like the claws of a diving osprey, before she figured out why the woman hadn't:

She was too busy talking to Jess.

## 3

...who could barely stand, now, whose knees dragged earthward as though they had magnets in them, whose splintered ribs were poking at least five distinct shards deep into her lungs, which didn't seem to be catching any of the air she kept trying to suck down. Ever since they'd left the apartment—really, since the moment the woman had clubbed her to the bedroom floor—Jess had been trying to come up with any idea that might save them. *Had*, in fact, come up with one or two pretty goodies. The scissors had almost worked.

But now she had nothing. Wouldn't have had the strength to wield anything, anyway, let alone drive whatever that might have been deep enough into the creature before her to do enough damage. As in, more than a scissors through the top of the spinal column apparently did.

And so, for the last few minutes, she'd forced herself to focus, as ferociously as she could, on the woman's babble. On the fact that she seemed compelled to keep it up, for some reason. Maybe, Jess made herself think, if she could figure out what that reason was, she might gain some leverage. Something she could use. Or just cling to, while she watched her lover and her grandchildren murdered.

Grandchildren.

The word surprised her. She hadn't even let herself think of Natalie's baby that way until right now, let alone Sophie's. Not consciously.

And yet, that's what they were, as far as she was concerned. Both of them. Hers.

"What do you think?" the woman asked, herding Jess out of the moonlight into the criss-crossed shadows under the pier. Mist-clouds trailing everywhere, piles of kelp heaped on the sand like newly dug graves. The woman waited for Jess to turn before she gestured with the bundles under her arm. One of which—Eddie's, in his Baltimore Orioles blanket—stirred slightly. Not as much as it should have. The other one—Roo's—made a pitiful, squeaking sound. "I could string them up right here. And by string, I mean hang." Again, she paused; again, Jess suspected this was for dramatic effect.

*But not because she's enjoying herself,* Jess realized. *She literally knows no other way. Not anymore.* Carefully, she produced the wince she thought the woman wanted.

Sure enough, the woman smiled. "And by hang, I of course just mean in their blankets. Like little weaver chicks in a nest, see? Safe and out of harm's way. Unless you think I'll have reason to harm them?"

Again, the pause. Jess just left her wince where it was. Easier than reproducing it every few seconds. She glanced at Benny draped over the woman's shoulder. For a second, she thought his head had moved. But now she suspected the wind had moved his hair. Nothing more.

"Hmm," said the woman. "In that case, maybe I should just go ahead and bury them right here, right now. That could be the best thing for them, really. Maybe a mama crab will take them in. Turns out mama crabs are so much better at burrowing out of sight than you are. Better mamas than either one of us, I'd say."

There it was again. That curious quality to the woman's chatter. Audible just at the end of every phrase, like breath in a bottle when the note gives out. *Hopelessness? Was that what that was?* Jess couldn't have said for certain. But it sounded like hopelessness, and came accompanied, almost rhythmically, by the sickening clink of scissors against spine.

Jess was still turned halfway around, so the woman could see the grimaces she clearly hoped to elicit. And so she saw Natalie coming a split second before the woman heard.

Then the woman whirled, so impossibly fast.

So Jess did the only thing left she could think of.

4

The window, *Mother thought, letting her eyes linger one moment longer on the little mama's face. That's why she'd been looking there. There had indeed been someone peering in. And yet, she'd betrayed nothing. Was betraying nothing, even now, as though she actually thought Mother couldn't hear, didn't know. A formidable creature, this one. Clever little mama. It would be almost a shame, later, feeding her shreds to the sand sharks.*

*Mother let the little mama believe just an instant longer. Let her imagine she didn't hear those pounding feet coming up behind, loud as tympani blasts even over the churning waves, the mindless, effortless, useless roar of the world.*

*Only as she turned did she allow herself a grin. Thinking,* Okay, fickle, fearful little mama's daughter. Imaginary, accidental Destiny, who stole my lover. Come to Mama....

## 5

Even in mid-air, Natalie wondered whether she'd been suckered and the Whistler's woman really had heard her. Then she wondered what the hell her own mother was doing, diving like that at the woman's knees. Then she saw the woman start to tip backward, and had to adjust at the last possible moment.

But she managed. Catching Mother about the shoulders as she tumbled over Jess's back, Natalie dragged her the rest of the way supine. The woman's arms jerked up, and both bundles she'd been carrying flew from her, one smacking into the sand a few feet away while the other hit the nearest piling with a wet splat. Benny's limp form, meanwhile, had slid down onto the woman's chest, and it pinned her long enough for Natalie to get her own feet under her, shove that squishy sound out of her head for just a few moments more, and drop down beside her.

*Same motion as CPR*, she thought as she drove her head downward like a chicken after seed. *Check the airwaves for breathing. Then head tilt, chin lift…*

A long time went by before Natalie even realized she was growling. Or purring. Had been the whole time, as she tore Mother's throat completely out and then kept right on going, submersing her whole face in blood, *so much blood, so cold, so still, so deep, like a dead pond.* Natalie had no need to breathe, experienced no compulsion to, but even still, the whole experience felt way too much like drowning. Seized every muscle she wasn't consciously commanding and locked it. It took all the remaining will she had to ignore the urge to get up, get away, grab her babe and *run*, but she forced herself to stay put, push deeper, gnashing at every squirty tendril of anything she encountered, until, with a clank that jarred her whole jaw, her teeth hit metal.

Even then, she kept grinding a little longer, severing, finishing. Gnawing around the metal blades.

*Scissors?*

When at last she straightened—*after, what, thirty seconds? Less?*—she saw her mother, half-prostrate, pulling herself with one arm over the sand toward the kid who *hadn't* hit the dock piling, using the other arm to clutch a wrapped bundle to her breast.

*A bundle that whimpered? Had it really?* Natalie couldn't tell for certain over the boom of the surf, and she couldn't see clearly through the patchwork quilt of floating mist and dock shadows and moonlight, had to suck furiously at the froth around her lips and coating her teeth before she could even call out. Still gurgling in frustration, anguish, terror, and maybe, just maybe, relief, she kneed Mother's corpse aside, and Benny's just-stirring form along with it, and scuttled toward Jess and the children. She had her hands out again. Was going to rip whichever kid that was right out of her mother's hands, because the other one was face down where he had landed, but that one was *definitely* screaming—when she heard something splinter directly overhead. Instinctively, she ducked, thinking some piece of pier might crash down.

Then she heard the grunt. In that voice. So familiar. As familiar as her own child's. As, of course, it should have been, because she'd known it so much longer. Almost all her life.

Kneeling there, the mist flowing around her, Natalie half-believed she even recognized the displacement in the air, the precise weight of Sophie's torso as it tumbled into view and plummeted to earth. It landed not twenty feet away with a quiet thud—*too quiet, so much quieter than that little bundle smacking against the piling moments before*—and, for one absurd second, it stuck upright in the sand, arm out, eyes still open. As though Sophie'd simply jumped feet first and plunged waist-deep but no deeper. As though there really were still legs under there.

Then Sophie's body tipped forward. One arm still flung out. Fingers still twitching. Still twitching.

*Not twitching,* Natalie realized, letting loose a sob but somehow choking back a scream. *Still scrabbling. Because Sophie was still in there.*

Or. Thing-Sophie was still in there. Alligator-Sophie. The thing that had been Sophie, and now was something else.

As Natalie watched, Sophie's head lifted slightly. Tilted over on her broken neck, so that Natalie could see her face. Lips working uselessly, like a fish gulping at the air.

But calling for her, Natalie knew. Even without sound. Or hope. Or legs. Reaching for her friend. Calling her name.

Tears in her eyes, scream still in her throat like a peach pit she would never again dislodge, Natalie turned away. Turned for the children.

6

Jess had heard the slobbering, slurping sounds her daughter made as she sucked that woman's life—if you could call it that—out of her clearly enough. She'd heard the thud as Sophie's body hit, too. But she never even glanced in that direction, couldn't have cared less what it was, didn't spare so much as a thought on figuring it out. She just kept digging her free hand into the sand, pulling herself sideways toward that squawking, squirming bundle not more than ten feet from her grasp. She did, however, pause just long enough to peer into the blanket she'd already collected. And another to close her eyes, for a, silent, screaming second.

And that was all the time the Whistler required, having already shimmied down a piling, to take stock, see what needed doing next, and lift the squirming bundle away just as Jess reached it.

## 7

*So perfect. So, so perfect. More perfect than he could possibly have dreamed dreamed dreamed, let alone orchestrated. Like in a song. A song he could have written himself, and maybe he should start writing them, now, instead of just singing them. His Destiny's child in his arms. His Destiny's mother at his feet, at his mercy, supplanted already in the rush of fated love that not even death could deny. Moonlight and mist everywhere. The empty beach blank, awaiting racing lovers' footprints. His old, cruel lover's corpse, with its lifeblood leaking into the living, wriggling sand. His Destiny herself kneeling there, having already, by her own hands—teeth, anyway—freed him. So that she could be his, be his baby. His one and only baby.*

*But not quite yet. There was one step more. And even that lay mapped out so exquisitely before him. His Destiny had even left him a role to play, though she'd never admit to intending it. A role only he could play, one only he would have the courage to fulfill. God, but he loved her already. Would show her the wonders of the nightworld as they fled forever down its face, leaving their ghost-prints for the waters of the world to swallow. Leaving no trace but melody. A Whistling in the wind.*

*Planting his feet apart, ignoring the woman at his feet except to kick her aside, he stared at his Destiny where she knelt. By the look on her face, he realized, with a positively electric shudder, that she already understood. Knew, already, what had to happen next. What he was about to ask of her. Because she was a woman like no other. Was his Destiny, even before she was His.*

*Smiling—glowing, he was sure, like the walking, Whistling moon—he freed his Destiny's child from its wrappings and lifted it, squirming and squealing, high over his head.*

## 8

"Finish," he said, holding Eddie—and it was definitely Eddie, Natalie could feel his cry all the way down in the soles of her feet—aloft in his blood-drenched hands. The Whistler had shed his sombrero somewhere, and stood before her, pale and thin, like a stalactite made of moonlight. He really was beautiful. Monstrously so.

"What?" she somehow made herself whisper. Pretending, for just a little longer, that she didn't understand what he meant. For her own sake, for her sanity, not because she imagined any tactical advantage. Tactics were over. The Whistler had Eddie.

"My Destiny," he said. "My poor, tired Destiny. Hungry Destiny. Eat."

"Who?" Natalie whispered. Out of habit. Stalling, just to stall. "Who should I eat?"

But now…good God…he was smiling. Starting to lower her son to his chest. *To hand him to her? So that she could… Did he really think she'd…*

Just in time, he seemed to think better of that. Pulled Eddie back to his body. He kept smiling at her, though. *Lovingly,* she realized. *Or damn near that. A perfect facsimile. Like his singing. Like* all *singing, really. The great approximation. Feeling without truly feeling. Feeling without facing what feeling ultimately cost.*

"It doesn't matter," he said. Reverently. "Just understand. I'm leaving you no more time. For your own good. It's time. Right now. My love."

He made no threatening gesture, just stood there holding Eddie against his heatless body. The threat entirely implicit. She would eat— Finish—or he would kill her son.

Natalie felt her gaze drift, helplessly, toward her mother, who lay buckled on her side where the Whistler had kicked her, Sophie's Roo close against her, eyes riveted on her daughter's. Those knifing, deadly eyes. That gaze Natalie had never been able to escape. And never seriously wanted to.

*Did she understand the choice being offered, too*? It seemed impossible to Natalie that Jess could. And also impossible that she didn't. Natalie thought about apologizing, just once more, for all of it. For the total wreckage of all of their lives. Her mother, though, would have told her not to bother. Because what could apologies possibly help?

And because Jess loved her. With a ferocity that had cost her most of her life, long before Natalie's idiocy had brought them to this beach.

*Maybe that would help her understand,* Natalie thought. *Surely, Mama. You would have done the same.*

With a glance Natalie hoped conveyed at least a little of everything she felt, everything she'd thought, she turned around and saw Benny pushing himself up off of Mother's body, shaking his head, half-collapsing as he rested on quivering elbows. Silently, without any more dithering and without glancing toward Sophie's torso—*still scrabbling, over there, hopelessly calling for her, in a gesture as inarticulate and unmistakable as her son's cry*—Natalie started on her knees toward him.

Her mother's hiss stopped her dead. Natalie turned. Saw her mother, who hadn't moved.

"Natalie. Don't you dare."

"Mom—"

"Not him. Do you hear? Not him. This isn't his doing. And it isn't his fight, no matter how hard he's tried to let me make it his. This is *your* fight. And mine."

"Mom…"

"Natalie," Jess said, in that voice that sounded so natural in her mouth, came so naturally, always had. Lips flat. Eyes tearless. "Come here."

*Where did that voice come from*, Natalie wondered? *And how do people learn it? Did I have it, just at the end?*

For a single moment, she wavered, watching Benny sag to the sand. Very possibly dying anyway. Then, not bothering to fight back her tears, she turned and did what her mother demanded. She managed to keep her eyes away from Sophie's, but she did look up, once, at the Whistler. His ecstasy had all but overwhelmed him. Set him hopping back and forth. A savage, singing leprechaun, holding the only pot of gold Natalie had ever known. Dangling it before her.

*Go ahead and dance,* she thought, savagely. *But be careful what you wish for. Because when you've given me back what's mine...when I'm Finished... by the time I'm finished with you...*

Somehow, despite audible cracking sounds from somewhere in her ribs, Jess had pushed herself upright, and as Natalie reached her, she straightened further. Even kneeling, Natalie was a full head taller. And felt three feet smaller. She watched her mother hold up a finger, then lay the little bundle in her arms gently in the sand. Hover absolutely still over it a moment, as though it were still Sophie's Roo, still a child, one she'd finally gotten down to its rest.

When she straightened again, Natalie experienced a single moment of wavering. A desperation just to get right up out of her skin and float away. Not be Natalie, anymore. Be whatever she was now, which could still be whatever she wanted. Stop being this woman's daughter. Her child's mother. The Whistler's Destiny, one way or another.

Then the moment was gone. Steamed away by the blazing, blue light in her mother's eyes.

Unless that light was her own.

"Mom," she said. "Are you sure?" A rhetorical question, she knew.

Jess didn't bother to respond. She shed no tears, offered no final remonstrance or last, completely absurd, reassuring smile. In front of her, Natalie saw only that relentless *will*. That Jess-ness. Natalie felt her own tears massing, and let them come. "I have...I *do*...love you. Mom."

"I love you, too," Jess murmured. Dead flat. "Hurry up."

But Natalie heard it, this time. The weeping underneath the flatness. Buried so far down in there, where it burned forever, never went out, like a pilot light. The frozen heat that had driven her mother forever forward through her days. All these endless, lonely years.

Natalie was bending forward, had already given her mother a farewell kiss on her cheek and slid her mouth down toward her neck, before she felt her mother's hands in her sweater pocket, and realized, all at once, what was *really* happening. What Jess had seen, and why she had really called her back from Benny. She glanced up then, and what she mostly felt was wonder. *How had her mother known? How had she understood so much about what was happening here? So much more, with so much more profound comprehension, than even Natalie had?* She had her cheekbone against her mother's shoulder, was gazing straight up into Jess's face as her mother pulled the gun from Natalie's pocket.

*How had Jess known? Because she'd seen the look in Natalie's eyes, that night she'd come back to the trailer. Had maybe seen Sophie's eyes through the window tonight. She'd heard Mother jabbering. Had seen the Whistler holding her grandchild. And had understood—completely—what Finishing actually meant.*

*And what Natalie's Finishing would mean for Eddie. Who had become the only thing that mattered, the moment he was born.*

Natalie felt one last, utterly primal urge to lunge forward, protect herself. She squashed it easily. Lay against her mother's cheek, shuddering. Sobbing. And grateful. So grateful. "Mom," she whispered, while her mother did, finally, just once, touch her hair.

"I know, baby," Jess said, the tears exploding out of her at last. "I know."

Then she raised the gun up under her daughter's chin, kissed her forehead, and pulled the trigger.

9

They faced each other, then. Silently. Mist floating around them. Jess and the Whistler. Seagulls shrieking, spinning out to sea.

*Carrying my daughter with them,* Jess thought, resisting the urge even to wipe Natalie's brains off her face. *Spiriting her away.* If she so much as opened her mouth, she knew, she would simply shudder to pieces. So she stayed still. Gun still raised, though not aimed anywhere.

Finally, after a long time, she started to order the Whistler to put Eddie down, but was surprised to find he'd already done that. Laid the bundle at his feet. Not gently, but not cruelly. The way one would a grocery bag. Because this wasn't about Eddie, Jess realized. Never had been. Because they didn't think that way, whatever they were.

*Which was why she'd had to…*

Jamming her teeth together so hard she felt the front ones crack, Jess somehow stopped that thought dead. Held still. Held on. Watched the Whistler watch her.

*At least it really wasn't about Eddie*, she realized. *He'd probably leave him right there, when he was finished with her. Someone would find him. Surely, by morning, someone would. All he had to do was hold tight.*

*And he damn well had the genes for that.*

And still, the Whistler just stood there, staring at her.

"Well?" she hissed, through jaws she didn't dare loosen. "Go ahead."

Only then did she realize that the Whistler *wasn't*, in fact, staring at her. He was staring at Natalie's body. And with a shudder, Jess realized she could actually see his feelings—if that's what they were, if that's what they called them—emptying out of him. Into his shadow, seemingly. Into the damp, drifting air.

After a long, long, silent while, he shrugged. "What for?" he said.

And then, with a sort of wriggle and hop, he was behind her, vanishing up the beach into the dark.

Jess had no idea how long she just knelt there, cradling her daughter's body. Singing to it, without even realizing it. Crying, though less than she wanted to. If she cried the way she really wanted to—if anyone ever did that—there'd be no more living. And there were still others, now, who needed her to live.

And so, straightening a hank of Natalie's bloody, beautiful hair around her ear, Jess laid her in the sand, ignored her own screaming ribs, and stood. Staggering, some, but continuing anyway, she shuffled forward to put Sophie out of her misery and collect what was left of her family.